LIFE IS A LOTTERY,

DEATH AN INCONVENIENCE!

My wife said to me: 'If you won the lottery, would you still love me?' I said: 'Of course I would. I'd miss you, but I'd still love you.'

Frank Carson

PROLOGUE

Many of us start off by really believing that some day our lottery numbers **will** come up.   We hear the mathematicians and realists telling us that there is a 40 million to one chance, or some such equally impossible possibility of success, but we know that if those people who did win, had been deterred by the same argument, then they would have missed out completely on a life-changing event.   The saying 'you've got to be in it to win it', despite all the pundits' sneering, is also very very true!   You may have a slender chance of winning the lottery, but without a ticket you have no chance!   That's why so many people, despite their decreasing faith that their numbers will ever really come up, still continue to try their luck.   The result of actually winning – at least winning big – is so totally life changing for most people that it is seen as worth pursuing however minute the odds.

On the other hand, death is not a gamble, it is the one big certainty.   No bookmaker would give you odds against your ultimate demise.   It is a no brainer!   We **will** all die.   No lottery in that.   The when, the where, the how may vary, but the end result is an odds on certainty.

Sandra Jameson had to come to terms with both: the reality of a lottery win, and the inevitability of death within a two hour time-frame!   She was in a great deal of debt; her husband was to a great extent responsible for her money woes; all her problems would be solved, in one fell swoop, by a big lottery win.   But … on the very day they won the lottery, her husband was tragically killed, aged just 48, in circumstances that, were they not so tragic, would be comic   - the stuff of a Monty Python sketch, perhaps!

What should be her emotions? What would be your emotions?   Honestly now.   How would you stop your mind careering back and forth between distress and euphoria?   Add to that the fact that the ticket is missing, last seen in the corpse's hand.   What then, my friends, how are you feeling now?   How are your conflicting emotions serving you?   That was poor Sandra's dilemma!

Chapter 1:   *The Funeral*

…...."and so we come here today to say 'au revoir' to our beloved ….   Simon …, who though moving out of our sight for a while, albeit with distressing suddenness, has merely stepped off into another room to await our own inevitable arrival...

There was just too noticeable a tell-tale gap before the name "Simon"   to really carry off the Vicar's attempt to give the impression that he was eulogising about a life-long bosom pal, or indeed, even a parishioner. Hardly surprising, since he had arrived at Sandra's door out of the blue, alerted by the undertaker, only 15 days previously.

Sandra had been deliberating with herself, and embarrassing friends and acquaintances, by bringing them into the debate as to whether Simon should have a 'proper service' or whether, as a many times avowed atheist, he should be laid to rest (or more accurately consigned to the flames) in a less hypocritical fashion.

So the apparition at the front door with his sturdy sit up and beg bicycle, his safety conscious disproportionately large black helmet, only challenged for attention by the severely pronounced cast in his left eye, mesmerised Sandra and took her by surprise.   Before she knew what was happening, the vicar - "I'm Nigel, from St. Barnabas up in Stanley Street" - was inside, cup of tea in hand, making arrangements for the service at the crematorium.

Sandra remembered chatting inanely, not least because she was terrified that she would be caught staring transfixed by the renegade eye, but Nigel put this down to grief.   He nonetheless scribbled away noting down little anecdotes for use in the service.   As far as Sandra was concerned, this was idle chatter, certainly not for public consumption!

At the worst possible moment, during the service itself,

Sandra would be made to rue her loquaciousness. The guests at the crematorium, not least Simon's relatives, might have been spared the insight into all the little foibles so irritating in the happy lives of Sandra and Simon Jameson. Nigel, who was obviously not experienced in these sorts of matters, but very eager to do his best, had tried injecting some intimacy and humour into the eulogy. Amongst other little titbits, he let them into the secret that Simon was an electrical engineer who, at home at any rate, was like most husbands, good at starting repair jobs, but seldom finished them; he was 'a man of few words' least of those being 'please' and 'thank you'; was, though, a splendid and reliable dog walker, who much to the suspicion and consternation of the neighbours and the local constabulary, usually did this in the early hours of the morning. Nigel made Simon seem about as much use as a Robin Reliant to Lewis Hamilton at Silverstone!

At the time all this was being said though, Sandra's mind was miles away. As she pretended to study the printed 'Order of Service' which told her that today was the 26th May, 2010, and that the cremation service for Simon Jameson – her husband for the past twenty three years – was now taking place, her mind, completely undisciplined and uncontrolled despite her present location, wandered at will over the past two weeks.   First a lottery winner, then a tragic widow, then a grave robber (well that's a bit of an exaggeration but its all in the interpretation really!), then a depressive, accelerating to manic depressive, and all this driving her to become some kind of Miss Marple, or Hecule Poirot.   Not driven, you understand, by pure interference and nosiness, but entirely by despair and urgency.   Indeed, let the person who does not think they would act somewhat irrationally under the same circumstances stand up so that I can either see a halo, or the forked tongue of a liar!

While the detective cogs were churning in the front pew of the crematorium chapel, the Reverend Nigel Smith continued, unaware that he had completely lost the widow, in mind if not in body, but was unfortunately stunning the other mourners into total incredulity and outrage.   There is certainly such a thing as too much information, Nigel!   Usually people, civilised people at any rate, tend to try to recall and remind people of good things about the dear departed, and not their bad manners, uselessness and strange habits!   None of the lovely, funny, warm and useful anecdotes seemed to have stuck in the Rev's brain at all, or if they had he thought those of lesser use for the purpose of this particular exercise.   At last he seemed to be winding up, much to everybody's relief and his closing notes could not have been more welcome, even if a trifle inappropriate.

There had been times through the eulogy when people could have been forgiven for thinking that perhaps he was a fraud, a shyster who had decided to use that particular audience to rehearse some new form of 'stand up' routine!

"The circumstances are, of course, tragic,..... (and I know the poor driver is devastated by the incident .... never before has a Toyota Yaris made such an apocryphal bid for freedom from the top tier of his car transporter) ..... but the outlook is indeed bright for Simon because he will now have peace and perpetual happiness.   (Simon's colleagues and neighbours in the congregation could not help but add as a silent rider 'whether he wanted it or not')!

And then it was finished, and as the sound system played (some felt quite inappropriately given the Japanese involvement in the tragedy) the aria from Madam Butterfly, the curtains closed against the coffin, and it slid into the awaiting chasm of certain finality.

As people left the building, they were duty bound to shake hands with a decidedly distracted Sandra, accompanied by her two daughters, who were traumatised by the whole series of events: their father's sudden and violent end, their mother's lack of focus and function, and now this 5ft 3in pretend vicar (who it transpired was actually a curate, and a very new one a that!) whose idea of comforting grieving relatives seemed to be as wayward as his eye.   The mourners, too, filing out were desperately trying not to look the Reverend Nigel in either eye, and everybody was visibly shaken by the whole service.   Though most of them put Sandra's lack of 'presence' down to shock, grief, and the nature of the occasion, they could not find any similar kind of excuse for the vicar.

Chapter 2:   How it all began

I despise the Lottery. There's less chance of you becoming a millionaire than there is of getting hit on the head by a passing asteroid!   (Brian May

.... or a flying Toyota Yaris, perhaps?   *(Elle Fran Williams!)*

"Tonight, thanks for Mr. Jeremy Stephens, of Solihull, we are using Guinevere, with set of balls number 4.

And the first one out is, for only the twenty seventh time ever, number 14; and the next up is number....32, last drawn three weeks ago.   Here we have a pink ball, it's number 3, drawn last Saturday and making another appearance tonight.   On its way is our next number, and it is 17, last outing for this ball was January 2007, so not a frequent guest.   Onwards now to the fifth ball, another pink one, it is number 4, last drawn seven weeks ago. Here now is your sixth and final ball, and it is a repeat appearance again from last Wednesday, number 48.   Your bonus ball this Saturday ..... wait for it .... is ..... number 44.

So there you have it, ladies and gentlemen, the lucky numbers for tonight, Saturday, 15th May, 2008, are in ascending order: 3, 4, 14, 17, 32, and 48.   The bonus ball is 44."

Had Sandra ever pictured this moment, she would have been leaping around, screaming wildly, rushing out of the house to tell anybody within earshot, or flying to the phone to share the news with the children. But sod's law being what it is, she was not actually there at the time that all this was unfolding. Simon sat staring at the screen, holding a piece of paper in his hand.   He was quite calm and seemingly unaffected by anything – even something as life-changing as this.   After a few moments of inaction, he finally stood up and calmly walked into the kitchen and just like saying 'the Germans have just beaten San Marino 8 – 1 again' which would hardly have been earth-shatteringly unexpected, he said "I think we've got all six numbers up on the lottery".

Simon was not a joker, normally, but it was a very, very crucial statement, so Sandra, like most people in her situation, spoke those universal words" Stop mucking about, Simon.   That's not funny!"

Though by his very nature she recognised that the likelihood of him winding her up was remote, she was still terrified to take him seriously. "With our present level of financial stress, that's not even funny – people have jumped off of multi-storey car parks for less"!

"No, darling, no joke – here take a look. I wrote the numbers down from the tele. We always use the same numbers, so I'm sure it's right, but you had better check them anyway, just in case, before I make a pillock of us with wishful thinking".

The use of the endearment was the only unexpected aspect of the statement. It was the single true sign of Simon's real inner feelings. His actual body language and expression, or really his lack of expression or even any mild excitement, completely belied his words. He rarely used any form of name substitute, though in actual fact he rarely used names either, and when he did use alternatives, he somehow managed (quite misleadingly as it happened) to convey the impression that he did so because he could not quite remember the proper name ..... just on the tip of his tongue, but not quite get-atable.   This time, though, he had used the word 'darling' almost naturally and hence quite unnaturally for a man of his introversion and normal total composure.

Just before Simon passed the piece of paper over to Sandra to confirm his own certainty and in doing so answer her prayers and open the floodgates to euphoria, the door bell chimed and in mid-movement he turned and headed for the front door, gesturing to Sandra to say nothing about the matter, just yet.

At the door stood their next door neighbour.   Nobody in the close was exactly 'borrow a cup of sugar' type, and it was not the sort of community that held wild parties, swinging or otherwise, but for normal everyday purposes everybody was on reasonably good terms. Some people were more gregarious than others, obviously, but even those less friendly by nature or preference, were still always happy to lend a hand in times of need.

"Simon, do you think you could give me and James a hand pushing Terri's car?   If we can get it to the top of the hill she can perhaps bump-start it."

"Sure Stef, no problem.   Just let me get my shoes on and my other jacket – is it still chucking it down out there?"

"Yes, you'll need something, but don't put on a good one, you know Terri's car is a proper Dagenham dustbin. You'll ruin a good one."

Sandra would be able to re-run this scene in her mind flawlessly – and she did so every hour on the hour for weeks after.   It was the last time she actually saw Simon alive.

Simon, Stefan and James trundled the old Ford Fiesta up to the top of the hill and, with Terri steering, managed to turn it the 90 degrees necessary to give it the best possible chance of a straight run down hill, along a less obstructed roadway.   The enterprise fared well, and mission was accomplished.

At the end of the road, just as the three musketeers were making their way back up the hill again towards their respective homes, they noticed, but paid little real attention to, a car transporter on the corner.   The driver was up on the top platform, fiddling with the controls which dropped the levels and tilted the platforms.   It seemed a very strange time to be delivering cars, but they assumed that the driver had been delayed in transit and had arrived after the car dealership opposite had closed for the night.   They thought nothing more about it, and continued on their way, parting company at Simon's gate.

When he got indoors, he could hear Sandra talking excitedly on the telephone, and apart from anything else, to give himself a chance to come to terms with these new circumstances, and to be annoyed in private that she was already blowing the gaff, he beat a hasty retreat, crucially changing out of his old Barbour, which was now oily, dirty and wet, and reeking of exhaust fumes, into a newer mac which he had got for his last birthday from Sandra. He called the dog to him, gathered up the lead from the hall table, and turned back out of the house to gain some blameless thinking time, doing his regular duty of walking the dog. He usually went out much, much later than this, but these were not 'usual' times.

By the time he reached the spot where the transporter had been, it had been moved – not far, just around the corner, out of the main thoroughfare. It had been pulled off the road onto an abnormally wide grass verge, which bordered a wildlife area constructed by the local council to try to give local children something to find more interesting than graffiti, setting fire to things, and generally causing a nuisance.

Following his usual routine, Simon motioned the dog to cross the road to the grassier side, where he (that is the dog, not Simon) enjoyed the doggy smells and the possibility that he might espy and terrify a misfortunate squirrel or some other potential small victim.   Simon ambled after the dog, and as he approached the back of the transporter, he felt, rather than actually saw, slight movement from the cars on the top level.   This was somewhat disconcerting, but he had the passing notion that he would not mind a new car, should one decide to land at his feet.   However he walked around to the driver's cab, and was relieved to see that, since a light was visible, there must be life inside.   He rapped loudly on the window and a startled face appeared, monkey wrench in hand for protection.   He gestured to the driver to get out, which he seemed very reluctant to do.   Simon backed away giving him room, and led by example making his way to the back towards the rear of the vehicle once again, hopefully obliging the driver to do likewise.

As he got there, there was a slight noise, a slight movement, before a crescendo of noise and activity, as the leader of the pack – as it happened a gleaming black Toyota Yaris – plummeted from above.   Simon was mesmerised and his lack of instinct for self-preservation on this worst of all moments, gave him no opportunity to move out of the way.   As would be expected when several tons of steel, chrome, leather, rubber and sundry other materials lands on a 5ft 10 inch slight framed human being, much to the horror of the transporter's driver, Simon was killed instantly. The car bounded after hitting his now lifeless body, landing on its side at right angles to what would be any passing traffic.   The transporter driver was paralysed with shock, but eventually forced himself to check for vital signs, before ridiculously and pointlessly searching for his first aid kit from behind the driver's seat in his vehicle, then for swiftness used Simon's own mobile phone, which had fallen out of his pocket with the impact, and unlike it's owner was completely unscathed, to phone 999.

The driver took what seemed to the operator an inordinately long time to seek out road names and exact locations.   The road name sign had been the victim of an out of control car fire some months previously and had not, up to that point, been replaced. Eventually he was able to seek out the names of adjacent roads and give at least something to go on to the emergency services.

Though it seemed like an eternity, it was in reality only about nine or ten minutes later that he saw the first of the blue flashing lights approaching from across the wasteland of the wildlife area, and frantically waved his arms to give them quite unnecessary confirmation of the location.   Having reached the jumble of roads it would not have taken Martians, let alone the local police and ambulance drivers, much time to spot a car transporter, by now lit up like a Christmas tree, surrounded by spewn cars and dead bodies – well perhaps spewn cars and dead 'body', would be more accurate, but the principle remained.

None of this Sandra actually witnessed of course. Indeed some of the early part of the account might be wild speculation or poetic license, since only Simon (and perhaps the dog) were witnesses to the series of events in their entirety. However, piecing the picture together and using intuition, common sense and her supreme powers of deduction, in later speculative times, she would come to believe that the facts would not be a million miles away from those given above.

A PC and a WPC (Shepherd and Curtis respectively) had knocked on her door, perhaps twenty five minutes after the police had identified Simon from his driver's licence in his wallet, to give her the bare bones of the story, and to return the dog, who, oblivious to what had occurred, went straight to his bowl and started to eat his dinner. This was an irrelevant but significant fact which Sandra found amongst the most disturbing ones of all, since Simon had been devoted to 'his dog' and 'his dog' had been, to all intents and purposes, during his lifetime, devoted to him. Appearances can, obviously, be deceiving, but perhaps that was how the dog chose to assuage his feelings ..... comfort eating!

The police were very kind, somewhat confused – no more, no less than she was herself – at her state of mind and her very odd reaction to the news. However they had been taught at Hendon that people act very strangely in shock.

Her emotions ranged from horror to distress, to remembering the lottery, to worrying about the legitimacy of her claim (after all it was Simon who had actually bought the ticket this week) to guilt about even thinking about the lottery under the circumstances, and all imaginable stages between: best described as 'euphoric distress' – was there such a state of mind? It sounded amazingly close (literally translated!) to manic depression, but she was certainly not in that territory.... yet.

She was assured, of course, that enquiries would need

to be made as to how such a tragedy could have occurred; whether there was blame attributable on either side; whether there was negligence or vandalism involved …. She could not quite see how Simon could be part of the 'on either side', but did not argue the point at that juncture.

In the meantime, they told her that Simon had been taken to the hospital, though he had been pronounced dead at the scene.   He would most likely be moved to the hospital morgue to await a post-mortem, which would help to inform the subsequent enquiry and investigation.   In addition to the disappointed dog, who had obviously not had a very satisfactory walk, much to Sandra's relief they had also returned Simon's wallet and for some strange reason, one shoe.   She had to surmise that he must be wearing the other one?

Before they left, they enquired whether she wished to be taken to the mortuary, or whether she wished them to contact a relative or friend to be with her.   They almost visibly heaved a sigh of relief when she declined and very purposefully and pointedly putting their hats back on signifying that their visit was, therefore, at an end, they gladly left the house, having accomplished one of the worst aspects that their job can throw at them.   They were pleased with themselves, but were aware that what they had just witnessed was not really typical or representative … though whether there was any way of judging 'typical' or 'representative' behaviour, given such circumstances, it was difficult to say.   It was certainly not every day that one's husband suddenly met his maker courtesy of a Toyota Yaris, with no driver, no number plate and apparently no drink, drugs, excess speed or careless driving involved. Wrong place, wrong time, seemed somewhat inadequate as an explanation!

Left alone, she did not know what she ought to feel: To be a lottery winner and a widow in the course of two hours must be an unusual occurrence to put it mildly. She forced herself to sit down and be still.   She genuinely cried a few tears.   The sorrow was sincere, the shock genuine, but – in a way that nobody can really criticise until they have been in the same situation – it was competing only so-so with excitement over the financial and practical difference a few million might make to her life, and the lives of her children. She was concerned, too, that she did not really know where the ticket was at this precise moment. She assumed, and of course hoped, that it was nestling in the wallet safe and sound; a wallet even now beguiling her from across the room on the sideboard. Even though she was completely alone, she felt it showed too little feeling to rush to open it, having just received such terrible news. She forced herself to exhibit what was surely the normal, natural reaction at such a moment LOSS, rather than whoop over GOOD FORTUNE!

She crossed the room, finding it impossible not to look at the wallet, sitting innocently enough not ten feet away. It appeared, in a bizarre way, to be bathed in a spotlight created by the adjacent table lamp – like the opening act at the London Palladium, or indeed a scene from an old movie where good cop/bad cop were grilling a suspect to get a confession. Would the wallet cough up the ticket willingly? Would it give name, rank and lottery number?

Eventually she picked up the phone – she had better at least tell the children – and oh my goodness, Simon's family. She first of all rang Simon's brother, Nicholas, who had, much to her relief, undertaken to break the terrible news as gently as possible to his aged and ailing mother, Frankie, and the rest of the family. She then rang her own daughters: Sage was just finishing her first year at university in Exeter, and Amber was spending her gap year au pairing in Seattle. They were obviously distraught and were only persuaded with difficulty not to immediately return. She explained that because of the somewhat unusual circumstances it would perhaps be some time before all the investigations had been completed and she would not know anything or be able to plan further until everything was done and dusted. She had an awful thought as she spoke to them, that she had no money

to pay for even the most basic funeral ... unless ......
but she could not let herself think of either scenario —
the plight of the pauper and the pauper's grave, versus
the no expense spared, gold plated coffin, a carriage
pulled by horses with black plumes, or a burial at sea
on the most expensive hired yacht imaginable.   To do
so was the way to madness!

Sandra had lived with the worry of losing everything for
a very long time.   She had carried this burden alone,
not because she was the only one affected or even
responsible, but because she was the only one adult
enough to even try to pick up the pieces of see the
inevitability of their future collapse.

Simon had been, to all intents and purposes, a good
person.   He had had a somewhat sad early life, having
been brought up by his mother, the redoubtable
Frankie, without a father who had left the family home
when Nicholas was three and Frankie was pregnant
with Simon.   Both he and Nicholas had spent quite a

bit of their young lives in an out of care because of bouts of depression and inability to cope on the part of their mother. She had not married the boys' father, and the relationship had not been sanctioned by her parents, so when he left she was quite alone in the world. She had been brought up in a money rich, but affection poor household and sent off to boarding school at the age of 7 and 'finishing school' at the end of her formal education, during all of this time, despite not being stupid, she had gained some academic qualifications, but absolutely nothing that prepared her to cope with everyday life. That circumstance alone was probably responsible for a lot of the future trauma that she and the boys suffered. Having met Nicholas and Simon's father, Guy, literally on the train as she returned from school in Geneva, she had been swept off her feet by a rogue who believed that he had found the key to a life of plenty. She was besotted with him, and would not have a bad word said about him, and there were plenty said, by her parents. Eventually they gave her an ultimatum, him or them. Much to his concern, she chose him, but he still believed that they would come around in the end and all would be well.　When it did not, even when Nicholas was born, Frankie went through a couple of years of hell during which time Guy came and went as he saw fit until he finally ran out of patience when she became pregnant with Simon, so he decided to cut his losses and decamp before he had yet another mouth to feed. Frances (Frankie as she is now) had never learned really to earn a living, or even keep house, so everything came as a complete shock to her.　She wanted to care for the boys; she wanted to provide a nice home; she wanted to be able and practical and providing, but she just did not have the necessary building blocks to do so, and when times got really hard, she just fell to pieces and each time that happened the children ended up in care.

So Simon had not had the best of starts in life, but far from this making him more anxious to hang on to what he had, it simply made him believe that today was the only day that mattered and it was a case of carpe diem, but not in an entrepreneurial way but in a 'we should all do what we would like to do today and let tomorrow look after itself' kind of way.

He could be single-minded, to the exclusion of everything else, for instance when concentrating on an intricate piece of circuitry or a complex electronic conundrum.   When they had first married and before they had a family, they had lived in a flat which had a balcony.   He would sit for hours on that balcony, at a workbench intent on mending, or making, or improving some piece of electronic gadgetry.   On more than one occasion, during those days, women who could look across the wide courtyard from their window and see this paragon working away, would knock on Sandra's door and tell her how lucky she was to have him. They were in compete admiration to see a man content to be at home and not drinking, gambling or womanising and they frequently told her so in almost hushed and reverent terms.   They had no idea how many times Sandra weighed up the real merit in these comparisons.   It was of course very true and a very erudite observation, but it lost its 'admirability' to a huge extent when bills were left, relationships ignored and earnings spent on transformers, oscillators and soldering irons!

Simon was certainly not demanding, or violent, or even argumentative.   He was most of the time quite silent. He most certainly had loved his children, and given the right opportunity might even have died to protect them, but he could not communicate with them on a day to day basis.   He was not unpleasant or mistreating of them – or anyone – he was just mentally absent whilst physically within their sight.   That was difficult to understand for children and impossible for Sandra to try to explain to them, or anybody else.   If a person seems to be moaning about the absence of something, then they are most often criticised rather than comforted since people see the presence of 'bad' as worthy of sympathy and help rather than the absence of 'good'.   People generally merely comment that 'they don't know how lucky they are!'   People can see bruises, scars, even a broken or cowed spirit, because it usually is caused by some kind of 'action'.   It is less easy to understand the psychological damage done because a person does not do something, or worst still does not do anything!   So to put not too fine a point on it, whilst showing a smiling face to neighbours, children, work colleagues, Sandra had been battling bailiffs, debt collectors, bank managers, mortgage providers for a very very long time.

In some ways she realised she had only herself to blame.   Simon would have been perfectly happy in a rented bedsit, minus children, pets or friends, so long as he had space for a workbench and an electricity supply.   Sandra had seen this too late and had fallen into the trap that is laid for people who believe that everybody must aspire to exactly the same set of aims and achievements.

So, unfortunately under the current circumstances, one of the first direct debits to be stopped when they started to get into 'financial difficulties' was the endowment policy, swiftly followed by the life insurance policies, swiftly followed by anything else that would have been of assistance now!   It was not that they had been profligate in the conventional sense of the word.   Neither of them smoked, nor drank to excess, but her wage did not go far with a hefty mortgage, Council Tax and Services, not to mention putting food on the table, and Simon's salary never seemed to make it much further than paying off the many credit and store cards that he had accumulated over time in order to become the pride owner and user of some very sophisticated electronic gadgetry and test equipment.   The children had never gone without and probably had no idea, particularly now that they were living elsewhere, that things were as bad as they were. Luckily any time that a bailiff had knocked on the door she had been on her own.   If they had ever come when she was out and Simon was in, she could not say. He had never mentioned it, but he would have been oblivious to the consequences of such an occurrence in any case and most likely would not have answered the door, not because he thought it would be a bailiff, but because it was somebody …. anybody … he did not really like people when he was engrossed, and that was most of the time. He did come out of his shell sometimes, usually when he was privately celebrating having figured out or solved something, or achieved something, so on those few but memorable occasions when a party, or a gathering, coincided with such a frame of mine, he could surprise people by being chatty and sociable. Those times were rare, but were sufficient to give the neighbours the impression that 'he was an odd fish, but not so bad when you got to know him'! Hence they still felt they could knock on the door and ask for his help, for instance, pushing a car, or even more mending something! That kind of occasion was bliss to Simon, unless it was mending something within their own house, in which case, like the shoemaker's children who went unshod, so there were countless things around the house in need of repair, and if something needed mending, even something electrical, nine times out of ten, it would be Sandra who was seen with a screwdriver in her hand.

So anybody who has been inclined to think negative

thoughts about Sandra and her lack of consistent grief and heartbreak, should remember the old Indian proverb about walking in other men's shoes.... or in this case other women's shoes.

During the phone calls to both of the girls, she never mentioned any of these worries, nor the possible marvellous alternative sitting in the wallet, but she just wiped their tears metaphorically down the telephone lines, and promised she would keep them informed. She said to Amber in particular that she did not think that she should come back from America for the funeral, because it was a very expensive fare, and would serve no real purpose.   She said her Dad would understand, and would reiterate what Sandra was saying, if he was there.   Amber did not argue the case, but even at 19 she was old enough to know that if at all possible, she should, and would, return home, not least to be with her mother at such a horrible time, and definitely not leave it all to Sage.

Those necessary and unpleasant duties accomplished, she rubbed her sweaty palms down the sides of her faded denim jeans and with as much composure as she could muster, casually reached for the wallet. With trembling fingers she pulled out Simon's driving license, catching sight of his photo which gave her a pang of real sorrow, guilt, and not the smallest amount of embarrassment; two twenty pound notes, one fiver; an assortment of credit and store cards; various receipts and credit card slips; two books of stamps; several car park tickets and.... NOTHING!

Chapter 3:   *The lost millions!*

Following the untimely death of Simon Jameson, the next couple of weeks for those left behind were hectic to say the least. People do say that the grief over a loss cannot really begin until after the funeral, since there is just too much to do before then.   Everybody tried to be helpful, to take some of the weight and involvement off of Sandra's shoulders, but she seemed like a person possessed, and blocked, sometimes politely, sometimes not so politely, every attempt to share the burden.

Nicholas, who was inclined to be moody and ill-tempered at the best of times, was particularly critical, but naturally did not think he would gain many disciples by openly haranguing the grieving widow. There was, to add spice to the recipe, a history between them in any case.   Both of them knew this, neither of them every spoke of it, either between themselves or with others.   Nicholas had made several ham-fisted plays for Sandra before she married Simon, and was not used to losing out to his younger, and decidedly taciturn, brother.   More embarrassingly, he had tried twice or three times since then, whilst drunk at family Christmases and gatherings.   Drunk, but not foolhardy, however, since he always seemed to create, or capitalise on, situations when they found themselves alone, but when he knew Sandra would nonetheless not be anxious to cause a family crisis by making a scene.

The truth now, however, was that Sandra was afraid to take a back seat.   She had to be involved.   Of course she wanted it done right, but she also needed to find a small, but perfectly formed, piece of paper, worth much more than its weight in gold!

In the first place, Sandra kept telling herself, like Mr. Bannering, not to panic!   It had to be around somewhere.   Just keep calm.   Though not religious in recent years, she now said a few – indeed several, constant, perpetual – prayers to St. Anthony, the saint apparently who finds things, but it appeared he was not all that concerned with helping Sandra to put worldly riches over human tragedy and family loss.

She sat alone each evening, having shooed everybody who didn't actually live in the house away often in a very cavalier fashion.   Sage, who had now returned from university, she obviously had to tolerate in the house, but was such poor company that her daughter usually took herself off to her room because she found sitting with her mother, but with no real interaction between them, very upsetting.   Though she had not been close to her Dad, she found herself more tearful than she had imagined she would be.   They say you never miss something until it's gone, so she felt perhaps she had underestimated her father during his lifetime, and this gave her a lot of heartache and troubled nights.

Downstairs Sandra drew up endless lists of places she should look, possibilities that might have occurred. Nothing seemed to be too bizarre or unlikely!   She was suspicious of everybody!   Her targets included: Stefan, Terri and James: after all they had been with him immediately after he left the house with the paper in his hand;   the transporter driver – it could have fallen out of Simon's hand, or pocket, or the man could have stolen it after he was dead while they waited for the police and ambulance; it could have been the ambulance personnel; it could have been the police .... or a passer by?   Perhaps it was left lying in the road? Could it still be in the road?   Could the dog have eaten it?   Her accusations and imaginings knew no bounds!

Chapter 4:   *The Talk of the Neighbourhood*

So calmly, she drew up a plan of action.   Seeing her lost in thought, people around her imagined she was depressed, sorrowful, despondent, but in reality she was more than anythIng planning strategy; making mental notes; trying to picture, in her mind, Simon's last hour ..... not as people might suppose his last horrible, crushing, fatal moments, but the time after he spoke to her in the kitchen clutching the piece of paper, until he ...... well until the end.   And even after that.   Who might have that piece of paper now? Anybody could claim it if they found the ticket!   Were there any checks and investigations carried out when somebody claimed a big lottery win?   She did not know anybody who had won anything bigger than a tenner, so she had no idea how easy or difficult it was to claim on somebody else's ticket.

Needless to say her strange attitude and very bizarre behaviour were first of all tolerated quite well by everybody.   The neighbours, her relatives, the dog, all seemed prepared, in the first place, to make allowances for her, given her loss, not to mention the nature of the loss.   But it was already beginning to wear very thin.

She was seen examining every blade of grass, every nook and cranny along the roadside where poor Simon had met his demise;   she was even seen scrutinising dog dirt along that road and adjacent roads.   As far as this nasty activity was concerned, Sandra had no real hope that if the paper had passed through the dog's digestive system it would still be decipherable, but she just could not bring herself to ignore the possibility, improbable though it undoubtedly was.

She surprised the police, the hospital, the ambulance service, the Coroner's Office, the undertakers – even the department of the Council charged with arranging for the streets to be swept – by what seemed to be an obsession, verging on a fetish to touch and hold Simon's clothing. They could understand that she was in a very vulnerable state, so tried to be sympathetic, but it nonetheless was most disconcerting that she seemed so insistent, almost threatening, in her determination to track down every piece of clothing, and have them all back – to the last sock and shoelace.

The time between a fatal accident and the consequent funeral is always going to be complicated and distressing enough, but Sandra had to add another dimension to the whole catastrophe.   She was by this time, given the prices she was being quoted for even the simplest of funerals, determined to find the missing ticket.   Even if she had been the most heart broken widow, which she had realised quite quickly she was not, she would have still had an all-absorbing necessity to find that source of financial comfort. When eventually she had both her daughters back home and witnessing her most strange and manic behaviour it became even more difficult to persuade them, and others, that she was not in some way 'deranged', though they obviously put this down to the suddenness and finality of the terrible circumstances.

Amber when she returned had decided after the first two days that she was going to seek the advice of their GP.   This was difficult, of course, because like most people in the country in modern times, 'their GP' was not a person but a practice ….. none of the practitioners within the practice really knew her well enough to be a real consolation or aid to any of them. They could mouth platitudes and suggest the usual sleeping tablets and de-stressers, but ultimately they merely gave the verdict that 'it was no wonder she was upset and stressed, she had had a terrible shock. Nothing strange about that.   People would just have to be patient.   Time was a great healer!'

Chapter 5:   *Grave robbing   …. well not exactly!*

Waking up the morning after the tragedy, Sandra had only one thought in her mind.   She was going to the hospital to search Simon's clothing, because the ticket just had to be there.   There was no other explanation – well not one that she cared to think about because the others would mean that the ticket was in somebody else's possession or had already been redeemed!

She arrived bright and early and having no other experience of hospitals, apart from the maternity unit, which was not even in the same building, her only starting point had to be A & E.   She walked up to the counter and was told, quite offensively she thought, to wait because the receptionist was dealing with another query.   Though she was not in the mood for waiting, she bit her tongue and decided not to make a scene. Had the receptionist known it, she was at that very moment in real danger of a start to the day which she would not have been expecting from a mild looking, small framed, middle aged woman.   Certainly Sandra was wrought up enough to have taken the reception counter at one leap and gone for the frosty, officious old bat's throat without too much additional provocation!

Eventually the woman stopped reading the pieces of paper she had waved at Sandra to prove how much she was being interrupted by her interference, picked up the telephone and made a call, carrying on a short conversation about a changed appointment, followed by a much longer discussion about the merits or otherwise of the new batch of Great British Bake Off contestants, followed by a catch up on the latest goings on in Coronation Street.   Needless to say Sandra felt justified in bringing her fist firmly down on the counter and saying "next time that will be your face, if you don't earn your wages, that, incidentally, I am partly paying for ….   Get off the phone this minute and do you bloody job properly!"

The receptionist immediately called over a porter who was standing chatting to a patient closer to the doorway. "This woman is being aggressive and making threats against me." Whilst saying this she pointed at a notice which was prominently displayed which gave an assurance that the hospital authorities would not tolerate and would take 'very seriously' any form of abuse, threat, or insult against its staff .... etc. etc. If she thought that Sandra would be petrified by the threat of either a 5 ft.4 ins. Ronnie Corbett look-alike, or at the prospect of being hauled off by the boys in blue, she had another think coming to her. Sandra eye-balled the porter and said "I demand to see the Head of Administration for this shambles now. I am here on behalf of the Regional CHC and am certainly not encouraged or impressed by the courtesy, efficiency or lack of professionalism that I have seen so far!" At this point, another senior looking woman, witnessing the tale end of the confrontation, joined in the contretemps. She immediately felt she had to ameliorate the situation since the hospital was in deep enough trouble already and its situation on the 'standings list' was distressingly uncomfortable. "Now, Madam, how can I help you? I am Daphne Lambert, the PA to the Hospital Administrator, and I am sure there must have been some kind of misunderstanding. What can I help you with?" Of course the receptionist who was not without intelligence, only any kind of customer service qualities or good manners, immediately realised that an 'official' visiting on behalf of a Government body was hardly likely to walk into the general A & E reception, let alone threaten to put her fist in a member of staff's face...... not really going to happen, perhaps! She stood back, eye lids half closed, mouth twisted in a bored and challenging fashion, defying her 'protagonist' to get out of the hole she was digging for herself. However, it was the porter and Ms Lambert who had turned ashen faced, since neither of them had been privy to the early part of the encounter and so had no grounds for making a judgement other than the words that the woman spoke in an authoritative manner! The porter immediately made a judicious exit, finding something that he just had to do that very minute. Daphne was certainly not in a position to call her bluff, since she could only go on her own experience of the conversation, and though at one point the receptionist tried to intervene and call 'the trouble maker' a liar, being shushed and glared at by 'her superior, Miss Lambert' she thought 'bugger 'em!' and left them to it.   From Daphne Lambert's perspective, to not take the woman at face value was just too risky.   She was certainly not going to take any chances by calling her bluff!   However, at that moment, with the red mist clearing quickly from Sandra's eyes, she happened to spot on a big board giving directions to various departments including the terrifying, but today welcome word, 'Mortuary'.   That was where the police had said Simon would go after A & E. That was where she was heading.

With as much ice as she could muster in her eyes, she looked straight at the woman and said "Never mind, I've seen enough.   Don't bother to escort me anywhere, I shall not need to see anybody else, my report is complete."   With that she marched away in a determined fashion, with the receptionist (sucking her teeth, and not at all abashed or taken in by Sandra's portrayal of indignation) and a flustered Daphne Lambert not sure whether to call her back, rugby tackle her to stop her leaving, or just be glad that she was relieved of the responsibility of soothing her ruffled feathers.

Even Sandra felt that she had perhaps got herself into a bit of a silly situation and was glad that she had managed to extricate herself without being arrested or punching somebody.   She made a bee-line in the direction of 'the mortuary' arrow.

Reaching the mortuary, she first of all quite politely explained who she was, and despite being told that it was not a good idea, insisted on seeing Simon's body. The mortuary assistant reluctantly agreed, since she had no right to forbid it, only advise against it.

When Sandra saw Simon, she was first of all upset. She had only partially taken in the fact that he was gone, and even less let herself actually acknowledge the violent and sudden way he had been killed.   It was not something that either of them had ever thought about or imagined.   They were not immune to the knowledge that accidents happen, they could even have predicted nasty motor car – or even plane – crashes, but only in a kind of academic and 'could happen, but unlikely' way.   They had had their share of knocks, bumps and even more serious mishaps, but those were the inevitable ups and downs of living in the 20 and 21st centuries.   This final curtain had certainly not been anticipated, not even imagined ever.   How could it?   Who would ever have imagined such a far-fetched scenario?   If somebody wrote it in a book, or a film, there would have been sceptics who would question its likelihood.   But here was the proof.   Here he was, on a mortuary trolley.   Dead.   Pale. Lifeless. Naked ….. That was when shock, grief, reality was overtaken by panic, disbelief and a sudden realisation of what she was actually looking at.   He was naked. He had no clothes on.   No clothes, no ticket, no money!

She burst into tears. The mortuary attendant was perfectly used to such a reaction and would have been more surprised if no tears had been shed. She had warned the poor woman that it was best not to view the body, but she also understood that for most people it was necessary in order to prove to themselves that it was real, not just some horrible dream. Some people preferred to remember the nice times, and to not see the remnants of what had been somebody they loved, but others needed proof, needed that horrible and overused word 'closure'. The finality of death sometimes needed to be witnessed not just reported on.

Sandra felt drained and rudderless. She did not know where to go from here. She suddenly had a thought and turned to the mortuary attendant and asked what happened to his clothes. These had been bagged up and were being kept for the time being until the 'case' was closed and a line drawn under it. Sandra was told that some were certainly within the hospital, but there might be one or two things remaining with the police, she couldn't say for sure.   Most of the stuff carried in the ambulance would have been deposited with …. the bod …. with Mr. Jameson … when he was brought into A & E, and would then have been transferred to their secure area sometime later on.

Could she have these?   They were important to her. No, probably not at present, but later in the day it was expected to complete the post-mortem, and then presumably if nothing untoward was found, everything, including the body, would be released to the family.   It would not be long now, the post-mortem was scheduled for 11 o'clock and by the end of the day, all being well, everything would be sorted.

Having made this definitive statement, which suited Sandra very well, she was suddenly thrown back into despair by the mortuary attendant suddenly looking less certain and with a frown and the beginnings of doubt evident on her face, she suddenly looked straight at Sandra and threw the first pebble of doubt into the pond of relief and calmness.   Unfortunately, the attendant then proceeded to expand on her growing uncertainty about the time frame.   She said that whilst nobody was expecting that any real blame could be attributed to the actual instrument of death, namely the Toyota, it was possible, indeed possibly probable, that there was some kind of negligence on somebody's part, so since where there was blame there was a claim, it was likely, perhaps, that there would be some kind of on-going investigation, and perhaps even some kind of criminal charge, which would affect the situation.   She seemed quite dithery delivering this change of opinion, and got more and more uncertain, picking her words as carefully as she could, as she saw the change in Sandra's features from calm, to surprise, to interest to ….. yes, was that anger, was it frustration, was it distress ….. poor Miss Attendant could see all of these, and was becoming fearful.   She was very much at home with dead people, but living ones were not her forte, and she had never really come to terms with any kind of interaction with them, particularly when they became emotional or 'peculiar'. She gamely continued, though, backing away towards the safety of the inner sanctum .... From the point of view of the medical evidence, though, that should be finished certainly by the end of the day. It was not at all clear what the police, or the insurance companies, might be wishing to do about the on-going investigation. She knew nothing about any of that .... and now, if Mrs. Jameson would excuse her, she really had to go, she needed to get ready .... very busy day. Goodbye.

And she was gone. Sandra was by this time in floods of tears: partly sorrow, partly anger, partly frustration, partly just weariness and increasing despair. It was becoming less now a question of the huge sums of money ..... the multi multi multi thousands, indeed millions, which were rightfully hers .... but the four thousand and seventy five measly pounds which the Co-op was asking her to find for the most basic of basic funerals. Where was she going to get that from? Wonga? She was not sure that a 'Pay Day Loan' was going to help her much. Obviously if she had the ticket, doubtless her bank would be bending over backwards to retain her custom so would lend her the money pro tem, but if she had the bloody ticket she would not need them to 'lend' her the money, since even the bloody Co-op Funeral Services would probably extend the hand of friendship to a multi-millionaire and give her a bit of leeway!

She then went to the police station and fortunately was able to collect the bits and pieces of belongings which still remained in what would have been the 'evidence lockers', though since they did not seem to be treating the matter as requiring 'evidence' they were happy enough to hand them over.   These amounted to one shoe, a dog lead, some tictacs, an electric screwdriver .... and NOTHING!

She went to the ambulance station, but was told, sympathetically, but none the less distressingly, that any items gathered up with Simon, and which found themselves in the ambulance, would have been delivered with him to the hospital. So what remained at the ambulance station amounted to NOTHING!

Sandra asked if it would be possible to speak to the ambulance crew that was on duty at the time, and she was told that they were not available, but that if she left her telephone number, though it was not normal practice, they would check with the dispatchers and perhaps they could give her a call. They were not wanting to further distress this poor woman, but equally, even if they were aware which of their colleagues were involved in the call out, they were not at liberty to set her free on them without checking with them, and their superiors, first. So she came away from the ambulance station again with NOTHING!

She had been out all day, and Sage and Amber were at their wits end when she returned. The funeral people had been ringing every hour on the hour, and they had no way of contacting her. She had deliberately switched off her mobile and had no intention of telling her daughters where she was going, and certainly not why she was going there!

Both the girls were angry because they had been so worried, and were vying with one another to shout the loudest and tell their mother exactly what she had put them through, by her thoughtlessness.   She did not ease the tension, or improve relations, by saying in a cutting voice, born of the worry, anger, sorrow, desperation and frustration she felt, that now they knew how she had felt every time they had stayed out all night, gone off for hours on end, or stormed out of the house to who knew where, or with whom!   That they should grow up and realise that she had a life too, and that she did not have to explain her movements to them or anybody else!   This just proved to the girls how 'ill' she was since nobody could be that unreasonable and uncaring of their concern, if they were in their right mind, could they?   Suffice it to say, that neither of them had taken on board any of the 'truths' that Sandra had blurted out in her diatribe, since neither of them recognised any of those 'truths' as relating to them in any way whatsoever.   They would need to ring the doctor again.   More sedatives, perhaps, or did she need a spell in hospital? ..... Even the girls baulked at the thought of putting their mother on a psychiatric ward, but it was touch and go, and they discussed that it might be necessary in the end, to save her from herself, because she just was not right.... just acting really strangely.

Nobody was acting sensibly.   If Sandra had had any sense, she would have told the girls the whole story, and cleared the air, but she was convinced that the world at large, including her nearest and dearest, would condemn her out of hand for even thinking about a lottery ticket when her husband was lying dead on a trolley in a cold mortuary.   How uncaring must she be.   What kind of a monster was she?   No, she could not tell anybody.   She would be mortified.   She knew how she SHOULD feel, but the pull of not having to worry ever again about anything financial, and to be able to say to the Co-op, do your damnest and let Simon go out with all the whistles and bells, in a gold plated coffin if one is available, would be just wonderful.   It seemed to crowd out any other thought or consideration.   She must be a monster.   What kind of a human being could she be!   No, this had to remain her problem.   Nobody would understand – how could they?   It was not understandable!   So she soldiered on alone, not far from being considered sectionable by those same nearest and dearest!

Chapter 6:   *Where to look next?*

She lived, slept, ate, drank the puzzle for all of the intervening time between 'the catastrophe' and the funeral, and well beyond!

She totally alienated all of her neighbours, by visiting Stefan and Terri and grilling them about what Simon had been wearing and what they remembered of that night.   Sandra somehow made them feel that she was blaming them for the terrible accident, since if he had not been dragged out of the house to push the car, he would be safe and sound now.   Because she could not explain that it was not really Simon she was interested in (how sick would that have sounded to virtual strangers?) but the lottery ticket, in her prevarication, embarrassment and doubt, she merely sounded angry and accusing.   Though they were obviously sympathetic and, to some extent, understood that 'it was a difficult time' for her, she nonetheless irritated and alienated them.   Worst still, not only those immediate neighbours, but in the close knit world of 'close life', and more particularly by virtue of the Chinese whispers phenomenon, by the time it had reached the far reaches of the main road, the word was that she had pointedly accused Stefan and Terri of deliberately luring him to his death, and then leaving him bleeding on the floor whilst they strode home and drank wine.

She was her own worst enemy, it had to be acknowledged, but fate and the human condition did not make her situation any less fraught.   That being said, she actually did not know what 'the word on the street' was, and probably even if she did, it would have still played a very minor part in her worries and concerns.   A very minor role indeed.

So having failed to move any further forward by third degreeing the neighbours she had to take stock. What she did know now, however, was that Simon had been persuaded (was that significant?   Was that a deliberate ploy?) to take off his good jacket, and put on an old one.   She had not known about 'the switch' before her talk with Stefan.   She was not sure which 'old one', because Simon's clothing was still at the hospital.   So … could Stefan have   'acquired' the ticket in the change of clothing?   Why had he been so concerned about it anyway?   She did not go about advising her neighbours on their wearing apparel, so why the interest?   Why the concern?   It was decidedly suspicious.   She had not noticed that they were spending a lot of money lately, but then she had not, until now at any rate, thought to be particularly on the look out. In any case, they would 'stash it away' in the short term in case they looked suspicious.   If they moved away any time soon, she would know!

The next morning, as she set off for the hospital hopefully to collect Simon's belongings and to hear the unfortunate news that the body was being released to the undertakers (unfortunate because that would start the process off and they would need their money before too long!), she saw a man putting up a sign at the edge of next door's garden: *For Sale …. Eliades and Co.*   Well, now she knew, didn't she!

She was now not sure whether to go on looking, or to accost Terri, or to go to the police, or to telephone and complain to Camelot …. was there no end to this nightmare of decision making!

She knocked on Terri's door, but luckily there was no reply.   Terri and Stefan were both, as was usual with hard working non-millionaires, safe and sound at their daily work: Terri at 'Hair Apparent', the local hairdressers, and Stefan at the Town Hall.   What would certainly dot the 'i's and cross the 't's for Sandra later on that evening was the sight of Terri arriving home in a new car.   Because Sandra was suffering from narrow vision, she would fail to realise that this was not a 'new car' – new to Terri certainly, but new in the sense of 'I have just won the lottery' definitely not. The 'Dagenham dustbin' as Stefan called it, had failed to start several times since the 'fateful night' and they had finally decided that it had coughed it's last.   The 'new' one had not been bought as the result of a lucky event, but from precious savings and holiday money that had to be diverted in another, and not altogether welcome, direction.

Terri's mother (Mrs. Goodwin) had some time before been diagnosed with Alzheimer's.   Quite apart from this necessitating a reliable car so that Terri could care for her, as well as hold down her hairdressing job, the couple had also decided to sell up and move closer to ease the burden and to prevent the necessity of Mrs. Goodwin having to go into a nursing home at least for the time being.   None of this was, of course, known to Sandra, who had her own overwhelming problems. Nor did she realise that all this time she had been living next door to the daughter of her favourite teacher. Mrs. Goodwin had, more than anyone, influenced Sandra to concentrate on her school work, get a place at a good university, and believe that she was as good as anybody.   Not an idea which came naturally to Sandra.   She had been brought up in a family that had no interest in reading, in education, in fact in anything except 'knowing their place' and 'not getting above themselves'.   An old fashioned notion even in those days.

Sandra's father had worked hard and given his all to an employer from the age of 14 to 53 and had then been 'thrown on the scrap heap' as they saw it, without a second thought.   Her mother had certainly never been expected, or perhaps even allowed, to work but had seen her role as keeping a spotless house, watching every penny, putting 'proper' food on the table even when money was scarce, and even if it meant going without herself.   She oversaw that they were all dressed 'proper', and to save money made most of their clothing which she then darned and mended until there was more darn than cloth.   Above and beyond all that she saw her role as ensuring that everybody behaved well, and spoke respectfully to their elders and betters.   They were an old fashioned kind of family.

Sandra had met Simon whilst at university. He was a technical support worker at the local school and they were introduced by a friend of Sandra's who was doing a post graduate teaching qualification and had been sent to the school on placement. Sandra had never had a real boyfriend, having become something of a serious scholar. She had always doubted her own natural ability, and envied those students who seemed to be able to sail through on very little hard work. The couple were married within nine months of meeting, without ever 'living together' as would be the custom now, and not even because 'they had to'. Sandra had just seen it as 'the norm': you met somebody, you married, you had a family. In that order. Simon had not been bothered either way. He had 'loved' Sandra in his own way, but it was as much a matter of getting it all over and done with. The expectation was that he should settle down sometime, and it would be good to have somebody to take care of him, somebody reliable, unlike his mother. Sandra seemed as far from his mother as he could imagine, so she seemed like a good bet. It was the equivalent for Simon of 'a safe pair of hands' as much as an overwhelming desire to marry her, or even to marry anyone.   It just, almost in a mirror image of Sandra, was another rite of passage out of the way, and ticked off in the appropriate box.

So since Sandra had married she had never known what it was like to have no constraints over money. Unlike her mother, however, whose husband understood their situation and was as conscientious and careful as she was, Simon had neither understanding nor interest in knowing the value of money, nor the cost of living.   Simon just knew what he needed and what he wanted, and if the money was there, or even if it was not there, he lived on the premise that 'tomorrow was another day' and like Mr. Macawber, something would turn up, and if it didn't, then Sandra would sort something out.   She had never been in a situation where she could be absolutely certain that when the next bill came in she would be in a position to pay it.   One should not judge her too harshly now that Eldorado was within her grasp, but not within her hand.

Reaching the hospital, she went straight to the mortuary, not needing this time to run the gauntlet of Miss Good Manners, nor Miss Daphne Lambert.   The woman who had been there before, who communicated well with the dead, but had difficulties when it came to breathing people, was not there, presumably they worked on a shift system.   That meant that Sandra had to explain who she was once again, but this time the attendant was if anything too forward and chatty.   She was not really in the mood for trying to remember what she had told the last woman, and merely played the grieving widow role and explained that the post mortem should by now have been completed and could she please have her husband's possessions, which had come in with the ambulance crew?

The man expressed a disbelief that she had not been given these before and said that surely there had been no reason to keep them?   Surely the Post Mortem had been a mere rubber stamp job, so who was the 'job's worth' who had decided that she had to make another journey, at this sad time, in order to get what was rightfully hers now in any case?   He went off and gathered the meagre bag of possessions, which seemed hardy worth collecting, and Sandra became embarrassed that she had now taken the time of two people to hold in her hand such a paltry parcel.   She hoped, however, obviously, that the parcel when really examined would not prove quite so paltry!   She was told that the undertakers had already picked up her husband and that he was now with them at the Co-operative Funeral Home.   Did she know where that was?   Was she all right to get there?   Did she need a taxi?   This chap was quite different to his colleague which, in her precarious state of mind, sent her off on another voyage of suspicion!   Was he nice, because he had already found the ticket?   Was the previous woman offhand and distant because she was embarrassed and wanted to get her off the premises because she had found the ticket?   Nobody was above suspicion.   Nobody was too insignificant to consider a thief!

She went off home clutching her parcel.   Anxious to rip it open, but afraid to be disappointed again.

Eventually she had to take the bull by the horns and she opened the parcel.   One old jacket, one pair of good trousers, two socks, one pair of pants, one t-shirt (with Who Knows Where?   Written on it!).   She was beginning to believe that even Simon from the great beyond was mocking her now.   For goodness sake could he not just give her a proper sign as to where to find the bloody ticket and not arse around!   Also in the parcel was a small plastic bag with 55p, a postage stamp, a resistor, a battery and a receipt from Maplins, all of which had presumably been in his pockets, and …. NOTHING!

So all avenues now, it would seem, had been explored. She was no closer to finding the ticket now than she had been on day one.   Further away, in fact, since on day one, she had been confident she would find it quickly.   Now she was losing momentum and losing hope.   She burst into tears.   Tears of sorrow.   Tears of Anger.   Tears of Fear.   Tears of Frustration.   Tears of Exasperation.   But they just flowed like as one emotion .... nobody could have separated out the individual elements from each tear that fell.   She just wept.

It was at that point that The Reverend Nigel had knocked on the door and the count down to the funeral that she could not pay for had begun!

Chapter 7: *After the funeral*

Her daughters were beside themselves with worry.
They knew that it was a sad time for all of them, and
had not expected Sandra to be full of the joy of Spring,
but her mood was so erratic that they were each
finding it difficult to cope.

They were cross with her because she was unable to
see that they had lost their father too.   They were
cross because she would not 'pull herself together'.
They were cross because they needed to get on with
their own lives and they could not do that with her still
so raw.   Everybody told her to 'cry it all out'.   What
did they know!   She cried all the bloody time and
surely after all is said and done, she should be getting
some kind of a grip on it now!   They had been
annoyed at first because she was manic, running
around like a headless chicken; cross, agitated,
volatile.   But not tearful.   Now, when they thought
they should be over the worst, now she decides to do

the crying thing!

After two more weeks, both girls were persuaded to return to their separate lives and with relief on both sides, they said their goodbyes to their mother, and each other, and they were gone. Sandra heaved a sigh of relief. But now she was alone. She had no family around her. She had alienated Simon's family because they thought she had 'briefed' the curate to expose all of Simon's weaknesses to the world. She had alienated the neighbours by accusing Stefan and Terri of 'killing' Simon. She had been less than welcoming and civil to the various G.Ps that her daughters had rounded up to 'make her better' so there was nobody left to either piss off or to befriend her.

It was as she lay in bed with no reason to get up, and with no intention of going anything that the postman delivered the umpteenth reminder invoice from the Co-op. She knew it was there, without even going downstairs to see what wonders had come through the letter box.   It had been quite a clatter, so she knew that apart from 'that invoice' there would be a whole host of others, plus lots of brochures advertising testers, oscillators, soldering irons and lots of goodies which Simon would have eagerly studied and mooned over.

Eventually she got up but only because she was beginning to smell, even to herself, and she knew she had at least to have a shower and clean her teeth. She meandered downstairs and with absolutely no enthusiasm put the kettle on.   While it boiled, she went back and picked up the mountain of post from the mat.   She put it to one side until she felt like tearing it up before putting it in the recycling bin.   She tried not to look at it because she knew she would see the dreaded Co-op logo amongst the pile.   She still had to put her mind to that ticking bomb, but today was not the day.   Mañana!

She made a cup of tea.   Leaving it to stew for far too long, not because she was busy but because she could not be bothered to return to take the teabag out of the mug.   It looked like copper by the time she had finished, and then she found that the milk in the nearly empty fridge was very off and totally unusable.   She threw the whole lot down the sink, followed by the copper tea and sat back down on the kitchen stool. The phone rang.   She ignored it.   Her mobile beeped. She ignored it.   The phone rang again.   Again she ignored it.

Wandering eventually into the living room, she picked up the post simply because she could not bring herself to ignore it any longer.   She knew she had to sort herself out.   She knew that the girls had been right. She new all that, but to know is not to do!   She did not know whether she was grieving for Simon.   She did not know whether she was grieving for what might have been.   She was getting more concerned now that she did not know and to an increasing extent she did not care that she did not know.   She had looked at the paracetamol once of twice; she had even looked at Simon's razor blades which were still in the bathroom cabinet.   She knew only too well that that was the coward's way out, but it had been touch and go on more than one occasion.   The only thing that had stopped her was the fact that her daughters would have her debts, including their father's funeral to face, plus her own funeral.   She could not land them with that, quite apart from the trauma to them of her taking that kind of action.   They would have to live with that for the rest of their lives, and would, wrongly, blame themselves for leaving her to her own devices.   No, she could not do it, though it had been very tempting, very tempting.

The phone rang again, but despite standing right by it, she just let it ring.   She had switched off the answer-phone, because she did not want to know who had called.   It was bound to be somebody chasing money. There was nobody else who would ring her now.   The girls would use her mobile.   No, there was nobody else she wanted to hear from, nobody at all.

She gathered her courage and picked up the post. There was now a whole big bundle, since she had repeated today's pattern of behaviour over many days. But she somehow found the courage to at least approach the pile, and carry them to the kitchen table.

She tossed to one side all of the obvious catalogues, brochures, flyers and charity requests.   She felt she was a charity case in her own right, though she knew that her plight was insignificant compared to some people around the world, but it felt bad enough to her. She put in a pile those she recognised as 'proper' mail. Some were scary, some were less scary, some under other circumstances would have been almost welcome.

The first pile she tore up without any care or attention, making sure that the names and addresses were obliterated, though quietly acknowledging, almost chuckling to herself, that if somebody wanted to steal her identity to take out a loan or a mortgage they'd be very disappointed and she wished them good luck with that!

Then she moved onto the 'scary' pile.   The bills she knew she had (included the dreaded CFS!)   Yes, there it was the familiar Co-operative Funeral Services winking at her, indeed scowling at her, form the table. She moved that to one side.   She knew what that was. She could do absolutely nothing about it, and what's more they could not uncremate Simon, so bugger off..... she knew she had to pay them, but for the moment what she did not have they could not have either!

There were several utility bills. There was an envelope which had a EE logo on it, and which gave her a bit of a jolt.   What had happened to Simon's mobile?   Her phone was O2.   Simon's was Orange, now EE.   The bills would be going out on Direct Debit, when there was money in the account, but this was to tell 'him' that he should perhaps go for a different tariff, since his usage seemed to have altered.   A bit of an understatement, she thought, but never mind.   Where was his mobile?   It had not been returned by the police.   It was not with the odds and ends retrieved from the police station, and it was not with the stuff collected from the mortuary.   Where was it?   Sandra went over to her own mobile which she was amazed to see still had battery, despite her forgetting more often than not to recharge it these days.   She had missed calls from both of the girls; she had missed calls from …. yes she might have guessed…. CFS; she had lots of texts, which she deleted without even reading; she had emails which she treated in a similar fashion.   She dialled Simon's old number and surprisingly it rang! Nobody answered it, so she left a vague message asking if they could ring her back. She did not say who she was, in case that put them off.   If they had cheek enough to be still using the phone, nothing would probably be beyond them!

She did not get a call back, so she tried quite a few times, before the phone eventually went dead and had obviously been switched off.   She contemplated going to the police to report the phone as stolen, but for some reason was not anxious to do this.   She realised she was more than slightly disillusioned that the police had made no attempt to contact her or tell her whether anything had been decided over the 'on either side' negligence or vandalism that may or may not have been involved in the accident.   She knew she should have pushed them, but since she had no 'insurance' to claim against: Simon was not insured, it was not a vehicle accident as such so she could not claim against their motor insurance.   She had been waiting for them to confirm that it was the transporter driver's fault, whether through negligence or mechanical failure, so that she could claim off of his insurance, or more likely his employer's insurance.   All that was certain was that it was obviously not an 'Act of God' so the insurance company could not use that as their usual excuse.   As far as she knew, God did not throw Toyota Yaris cars off of the top of car transporters, even if he was bloody angry with somebody and even if she was sometimes bloody angry with Simon, she could not see that with paedophiles and terrorists, murderers and rapists in the world, God could be that angry with a man because he spent too much money, or devoted all his time to trying to mend knackered electronic equipment.   The poor sod – HER poor sod - did not deserve that kind of end, and somebody should be responsible.

The arrival, or more specifically the opening, of the EE letter was a major breakthrough in her frame of mind. She had no idea how long it had sat there, but now that she had opened it and realised its implications, it had given her a new impetus, a new line of attack.

Sandra picked up the land-line and telephoned Orange to inform them that Simon was dead and that currently she did not know where the phone was, or who had it. Having not got very far because with the automated robot directing the calls, because it was necessary to know passwords and lots of other information that she had never made it her business to know.   She tried the same exercise online, but that proved no more useful.   It seemed impossible ever to speak to a person in order to explain the situation.   She had been told once before, by somebody, she could not remember who, that if you stayed on the line, then you would get a person, because they needed to free up the line.   She tried this, but her patience ran out before they ran out of external lines, or so it seemed.   She was a bit stuck now, so decided her best bet might be to go into the Orange shop in person and at least that would give her the chance to speak to a living human being, face to face.   That at least had the reaction missing for so many days – she bathed, dressed, and left the house.

The Orange Shop listened to her story like it was some kind of episode of Poirot or Miss Marple as she explained to them all the lengths she had gone to to see if she could gather up the belongings of her poor dead husband.   She did not explain why she needed so desperately to do this and they were left with the impression that it was some kind of journey towards catharsis – a kind of rite of passage in order to learn to live again. She did not disillusion them. They were better thinking that and being helpful, than thinking that she was some kind of nut case who had a mad delusion that she had won the lottery! Some chance! What lupin thinks that a likely story. By the time she came to the reason for her bending their ear on this particular day, they were only too pleased to help her. They were able to cut through the robot cordon and piece together the movements of the phone. The phone, apparently, was last active in Lincolnshire that morning, but it had not been used to make any calls. Any calls it received were accepted but then rejected immediately. They all surmised that this sounded either like somebody did not know how to use the phone properly, or answered the phone and then got scared and immediately stopped the contact. Sandra was now at a loss. She now knew that the phone had been, in fact, stolen – or at least taken away from Simon, either dead or alive. She decided that she should go to the police since she needed to be sure that the accident was actually an accident and not a cover up for robbery or worse! In addition, the police would perhaps be able to find out where the phone was now and who had it.

That was her next port of call!

Chapter 8:   *Accident or Murder, the waters get muddied!*

When Sandra arrived at the police station, as luck would have it, the same Sergeant was on duty and recognised her.   He had been very sympathetic when she had collected the meagre collection before, and so he was quite happy to listen to her and to try to put her mind at rest, if that was possible, as long as it did not take up too much time.

Sandra explained that the phone was missing, and the sergeant immediately to reached for an incident sheet in order to take details about the theft of a mobile phone – a very ordinary event, and one of the most common crimes in the United Kingdom and elsewhere. Sandra tried to explain that she believed that the 'theft' of the phone was just a side issue and that it now cast doubt on the whole matter.   She insisted on knowing what the post mortem had said and when there was going to be an inquest.   The sergeant thought it unlikely, as it stood, that there would be an inquest since it was just a tragic accident and quite straightforward, albeit sad and unfortunate. Sandra was reluctant to lose his goodwill because, so far, he had been the person who had shown most patience with her, but she was nonetheless taken aback that no real investigation was going to take place, and that Simon's death as the result of either malice, stupidity or negligence, was just being accepted as 'unfortunate'. Sandra asked whether any 'blame' had been attributed, and surely that was what an inquest was for? As of that time, she had received nothing from anybody to explain anything or even to give her details as to who the transporter driver was, and who he worked for. Surely that was her right to know those kind of details? If she had been insured, then the insurance company would have been only too diligent in finding out the details and apportioning 'blame'. Since the insurance company of the driver/company probably had more to lose, then there was no way that they would be pushing for more information or for clarity. Clarity was probably the last thing they needed or wanted.

The Desk Sergeant was getting wary at this point, and tried the softly softly approach, nodding sagely and telling her that it was still very early days and that all would be sorted out 'in due course'. As soon as Sandra reacted adversely to this brush off, he in turn got officious and all but told her that it was police business and he was not at liberty to discuss it with her. Had she known it, that was Desk Sergeant Frank Pickles 'normal' demeanour: he was good at his job because he could juxtapose George Dixon's 'everybody's friend' with Jack Regan's 'get out of line, son, and I'll do you' without a change of script or costume! Indeed, he was generally referred to within the station as 'Prickles'. This was not only because of his name, but more particularly because he had been compared by one young female constable to a hedgehog, 'cute, but spiky and covered with fleas'! He resented the fleas bit, but rather prided himself on the rest of the comparison, and never did anything to alter it, indeed quite the reverse.

As it is not too hard to guess, to tell Sandra that the death of her husband, whether by accident or design, was 'not her business' but 'police business' was like red rag to a bull and she also immediately decided that her 'nice' approach was not working and that the gloves were definitely off. She demanded, through narrowing eyes and with almost a snarl, to speak to somebody *more senior in position rather than age*, preferably *somebody who had some kind of ability at policing as opposed to pen pushing*. Indeed somebody *in charge* of her husband's murder. She stressed the derogatory words in her 'request' in the certain and sincere hope that they would hit home and hurt the pompous old duffer. She continued, telling the open mouthed official that whether by accident or design, and whether by manslaughter or murder, her husband was no less dead at the hands of a person known to the police who were doing absolutely nothing about it. Since the foyer of the police station was filling up, and she was getting support from other people sitting waiting, eventually a Detective Sergeant was found who drew the short straw and was delegated to sort her out. He led her through to an interview room, and as he was totally unfamiliar with the whole matter, he asked her to outline the background while he tried to 'get up to speed' on the case.

Sandra began by congratulating him on referring to it as 'a case' since up to that point nobody had done anything at all to make her believe that the police were taking it as such.   As she sat there and lambasted the representative of officialdom, she suddenly became aware that for the first time she was now thinking not of the damn lottery ticket, but the death of poor Simon, and she felt much better for doing so.   All that angst and anger that she had wasted looking for that bloody ticket, and so little real grief and sorrow expended towards her poor husband.   She felt ashamed of herself and promised him a better deal.   She would get them to properly investigate the whole matter.

The detective, who identified himself as Detective Sergeant Daniels, was actually quite shocked by the story and the fact that so little effort had been taken to keep the poor woman informed.

The investigations were indeed on-going and quite a lot of headway had been made.   There was a complication because the driver of the transporter was not local and understandably he had been so traumatised by the whole affair that he had suffered what had been described as a sort of breakdown. Sandra could not stop herself from saying that she thought that a very convenient state of affairs, but DS Daniels said that according to the file, the man had been a gibbering wreck by the time that the ambulance and the police had arrived on the scene.   They had sent local police from his area to interview him on three separate occasions, but he had been unable to remember, or to explain, because his nerves were still 'in tatters'.   He had never witnessed such an event before and it had, apparently, hit him quite hard.

Sandra was not inclined to show any sympathy for this

distant 'wreck' since she had to believe that he had been negligent and that his negligence had caused Simon's death, and that was why he was 'a wreck' now. She was inclined to believe too that his 'wreckage' was very convenient and somebody should explain to him that he could run, but he could not hide, and that at some point in the not too far distant future, he would need to face his demons (possibly in the shape of Sandra!) head on.   She believed that the police were being too soft with him!

DS Daniels promised her that the matter was of course on-going and apologised again for the fact that so little effort had been made to keep her informed.   Just as she was going, she said to Daniels "What part of Lincolnshire does he live in then?"

The man was taken aback, but said "Where does Lincolnshire come into the equation? Who is in Lincolnshire?"

Back came Sandra again and sat down, DS Daniels being forced to follow suit since she seemed determined that all angles had not been covered and obviously she had information that they did not have.

Sandra told him about the phone, and the last known signals from the phone were quite recent and they were definitely in the Lincolnshire area.   DS Daniels was puzzled by this, since none of the location details in the file – which he was careful not to share with Sandra – mentioned Lincolnshire: in fact it did not mention anywhere in that part of the country at all. Daniels was surprised that she had been able to get details of the phone whereabouts from the service provider and made a mental note for himself that she was either very resourceful, very persuasive, or a fanaticist!

His face said he was very dubious, so gave him the mobile number and suggested that he check it out for himself.   He promised to investigate and to let her know as soon as they had anything worth telling her. Like many before him, he could not make up his mind whether she was for real, or whether she was off with the fairies. He had to admit though that whatever her mental state, she was right that more effort had to be made to get to the bottom of the incident: whether pure accident or an actual crime, it should never, never have happened and the transporter driver should not be allowed to hide behind his 'stress' for very much longer.

She left the station eventually saying goodbye jauntily to the Desk Sergeant on her way out and pointedly thanking him for his time and courtesy. He had no idea whether this was genuine or sarcastic, because he had very mixed memories of the conversation which had started off sweetness and light and had deteriorated into acrimony very quickly, but he could not remember doing anything at all to bring this change about. Bloody women, neurotic as hell. He was bloody glad he had never married. Fancy living with that kind of stress – you'd never know from one moment to the next what kind of mood she'd be in.

As Sandra walked to the bus, cursing the driving rain, the puddles, other people's lack of direction when they collided with her,   even though it was she who was rudderless and distracted, she realised that her whole focus had shifted.   Suddenly she was not so disgruntled by the fact that she was forced to trudge through the rain and wait for erratic buses because she had had to sell her car for a pittance to pay the mortgage for a few more months.   Though she was still acutely aware that she had not the slightest hope of paying the Co-op and getting them off her back for the foreseeable future she was not in anything like the same way destroyed by this fact.   She still had no idea how next month's bills were going to be paid, nor the month after that, and after that but it seemed much less important that she even had a house and bills to find.   So what if she ended up in some bed and breakfast somewhere, courtesy of the Local Authority, or under newspapers on a park bench, she would still be alive, which was more than anybody could say for

Simon! All those financial considerations were no less worrying, of course, but they had become secondary – and a very poor second – to the obsession that now gripped her to avenge poor Simon. Over recent years, she really could not have said whether they were 'happy' or not, but neither could she categorically say that she had felt 'unhappy'. Frustrated and permanently worried about money, exasperated and envious of Simon's permanent state of separation and compartmentalisation, definitely, but 'unhappy' with the fact that they were a family, a unit, not really. So, even at this late stage, this eleventh hour, Sandra had at last understood that she had her priorities all wrong. How could a man be allowed to meet such an end, such a final and irreversible fate, and nobody – not even her up to that point – find it outrageous and criminal that it should happen? Worst still that people should shrug and just say, ah well, that was sad, wasn't it and move on with their lives. She was worst than they were, they were strangers to Simon, they did not really know him. She knew him, they had children together, and yet she had wasted all her energy, all her compassion on herself and her concerns over the bloody lottery ticket.   Let them have the bloody money.   What did it matter now.   But they would not get away with killing Simon and just move on with their lives..... even the villain of the piece, the transporter driver, with or without a fortune winning lottery ticket!

Chapter 9: *Tracking down the villain*

The next morning, Sandra telephoned the police station to speak with DS Daniels, but he was not expected on duty until later on in the day.   She considered just asking that he ring her back, but she was reluctant to waste more time and lose the momentum.   There had been too much dilly dallying up to now in any case. She asked to be put through to anybody who could look up some information in the file for her.   She was expecting them to say that this was not possible and that the information in the file was confidential.   She suddenly remembered the name of the WPC who had called on her with the news of Simon's death, and asked if PC Curtis was in the station.   She was in luck. Jane Curtis had just come into the station in order to finish up some paperwork prior to going off duty. WPC Curtis was surprised that the call was put through to her, being a relatively young member of the force, and not given very much in the way of 'important' issues to decide, she was not used to such responsibility.   Sandra told her that she had spoken

with DS Daniels yesterday and he had given her the
name and address of the transporter driver because
her insurance company were anxious to get the
paperwork sorted because they assumed that some
action would be necessary in due course.   PC Curtis
thought that was all perfectly logical, so when Sandra
went on to say that in the heavy downpour yesterday
when she had left the station, she had dropped her bag
and the paper on which he had written the details had
unfortunately become illegible the young constable
could not feel anything but sympathy and
understanding. So, could WPC Curtis please just look
up the file and let her have the information again?
Sandra promised to take more care of it this time!
Jane Curtis promised to find the information and ring
Sandra back, but Sandra did not want to give her the
opportunity to discover that perhaps she should not
give this information out, so thought it slightly safer –
not 100% foolproof – but slightly safer, to say that she
would hold on because she could currently only receive
incoming calls, because BT had restricted her service
because the bill was outstanding.   Not sure whether to

be sympathetic, or embarrassed, or condemning of this, Jane muttered an agreement and scuttled off to find the file. She seemed to have been gone ages, and Sandra was surprised that it was not on a computer somewhere, rather than a piece of paper. She hoped that the delay was not because WPC Curtis had become suspicious and had suddenly had the wit to realise that she should ask somebody in authority whether this was all right. Much to Sandra's relief, eventually back came the unwitting spy with the name, address and telephone number of the transporter driver.

It was only after she had put the phone down and gone back to her paperwork that Jane had momentarily wondered how Sandra Jameson was ringing her if she could only receive incoming calls? She assumed she must be ringing from a neighbours phone. Yes, that would be it. Nice woman. Such a tragedy. She felt for her! Back to the task in hand!

So far so good! Sandra wished, despite her previous change of emphasis, that she did have a car, because it would have been so much easier to undertake the journey with four wheels of her own, as opposed to relying on public transport.   She realised she had three options: first, train and then however else she got onwards from there; second, there was the old scooter of Sage's in the garage, though whether this was still road worthy, and whether her driving licence was sufficient to rid it – or even whether she was capable of riding it! - she was unsure; third, she could, at a push, ask Nicholas.   They had not communicated much since the funeral, and she had no idea whether she was still beyond the pale with her in-laws, but she also knew that Nicholas's loins would overrule his allegiance to Frannie's wishes, if push came to shove! He would still preen at the notion that she had to come to him for help.   He would welcome the fact that this made her beholden to him, and that would mean that payment might be exacted!   Well he could try!

Sandra went into the garage to have a look at the now

sad looking scooter.   She found a can of petrol (Simon
was nothing if not a meticulous planner) on one of the
garage shelves.   She tipped this into the machine, and
realised that it was very old, so needed a key.   Where
might that be?   She hoped that Sage had not got it on
her own key ring.   It would not be much use to her if
so..... nor to Sage come to that.   Sandra went over to
the small cupboard in which Simon kept spare keys,
spark plugs, fan belts (those were the days – old tights,
or in her experience sometimes not so 'old' tights, were
the more normal 'fix'!);   spare bulbs and fuses.
Thank you Simon.   There was a scooter key,
efficiently labelled hanging on a hook.

Having fully opened the garage door, she wheeled the
machine onto the short driveway.   God, this took her
back!   How long since she rode a bike, let alone a
scooter!   She remembered the old days.   Her little
scooter had been her pride and joy, but had conked out
more times than not, and had always chosen the most
uncomfortable and inconvenient places to do so.
Those were the days, eh!

Anyway, enough musing.   She said a silent prayer, and in an unsolicited fashion a picture of Simon popped into her head, laughing and shaking his head.   He would have found it amusing to see her, at her age, even astride the damn thing,   let alone planning to ride it half way around the country!

She turned the key and ...... nothing!   She tried again, click, ... nothing!   Did these things have batteries?   If so, then without doubt the battery was dead.   After all it had not been ridden for ages.   As she put it back onto its props, she did not know whether she was glad or sorry.   She had been skittish and excited at being extraordinarily brave, and very proud of herself to be intending to put the clock back twenty years, breaking out from her current careful, boring self.   Underneath that excitement, however, she would have lied if she had not also acknowledged that she was completely petrified at the prospect, and that her 'current, boring' 47 year old self was telling her that she was a stupid, middle aged, laughing stock who should know better!

She went back into the garage to see if she could find a battery charger, and some leads. She did not even know where the damn battery was on the scooter – or even if it had one – but it was no use knowing that information if she did not have any means of using that her her advantage. She ferreted around for fifteen minutes of so, moving boxes, looking into cupboards, behind tins on shelves, but was not being very successful. As she searched, the garage door had partially closed behind her, but she continued to search by virtue of the remaining light which filtered in from the now only slightly open door. She did not stop to put on the light, so was only aware that she was not alone when the light became almost completely obscured and she swung around to find Nicholas standing blocking the light in the garage doorway.

To say she was surprised to see him, was an understatement. Simon's family had made no attempt to contact her since the funeral, but then neither had she made any attempt to contact them.

So she thought that was probably even stevens. Neither of them said anything for what seemed like an age, but Sandra was the first to break the silence. In the absence of any plan, or even any real describable reaction to his presence, she did the 'English thing' she said "Want a cup of tea?"

Nicholas, equally ignoring the fact that they both now carried an awful lot of baggage and angst over old and even less ancient times, simply said "Coffee'd be good".

Sandra stopped what she was doing, and opening the rest of the garage door so that they were not both trying to occupy the same tiny bit of doorway, led the way into the kitchen, and set about the task of making coffee. This was really more of an exercise in diversion, since it gave both parties an opportunity to cover their mixed emotions: embarrassment, sorrow, shame, …. and relief that they were at least now in the same room.

Nicholas had been genuinely concerned about Sandra and how she was coping. Nobody knew better than him that Simon would have not left things financially on a very even footing, particularly since he would not have expected to leave so soon. He knew that Sandra had not had it easy over many years as far as being the main financial planner and juggler in the partnership. He had also known that he should lend a hand and see whether he could be of any assistance, but he not only had the 'baggage' of his past embarrassing behaviour, but also he had been bloody angry at that incredible eulogy at the crematorium. You could blame the stupid clergyman all you liked, but he must have got his information from somewhere – he had not just made it up...... Nicholas had to admit that it was much too close to the truth for him to have had a lucky guess, even if he had been some kind of malicious moron who just liked wrecking families and causing mayhem. But, thinking about it, he had quite seen how it might have happened, given Sandra's shock, she had been on her own, the girls were both away, she would just have bumbled on to the first person who gave her any time.

Yes, he could, in retrospect, see how it had happened. All of what the damn man had said had been true …. just not a good time to pour it all out!   But he could well see that Sandra had not 'poured it out'   during the service, but at a time when she must have been shocked, sad, angry, worried, vulnerable … all those things which made us all say things which we might otherwise think better off if we were in our 'right minds'.   Yes, having thought about it, he wished it had not happened, but, unlike his mother who was still seething and condemning of 'that bitch' he wanted to let bygones be bygones.   In addition, now that his divorce had been finalised from Catherine (or as Frannie would say 'the other bitch', though why she should speak of the poor woman in those terms it was impossible to say, since Catherine had put up with Nicholas's womanising for much longer than most women would!) he was free to 'look after Sandra' without any complications. No Catherine, no Simon …. Frannie was still a problem, but what she did not know she would not worry over, and she could not live for ever!

From Sandra's perspective, Nicholas was not the person she would have liked to have seen in all the world, but he was at least somebody, and somebody who had known Simon and who she did not have to explain things to. She had not liked the rift that had occurred within the family. She had never had the chance, not that she would have taken it had it been offered, to explain how the débâcle at the funeral had occurred, but on the other hand she had spent 25 years watching her tongue and avoiding walking on people's corns with Frannie and the rest, and it was a shame that at this time, when she was so very alone, the whole thing had blown up. So, as long as he did not get any silly notions, or misinterpret her hospitality as something else, she was only too glad to see him, to see somebody, to talk to somebody, anybody. If it was Nicholas, then so be it.

After a while chatting like comparative strangers and avoiding 'dodgy' territory, Nicholas got a round to enquiring what she was trying to do with the scooter. He had assumed that she was intending to see it, or perhaps Sage was going to take it and use it, rather than have it sitting in the garage.   Sandra made a decision – not really a decision rather a reaction to Nicholas pulling a plug out, and she immediately described the situation with the police and the driver of the transporter, the lack of any kind of feed back over any investigation that was, or was not, taking place. She left out any mention of the lottery ticket, whether subconsciously or not who could say, but she really thought at the time that she was now only interesting in the justice of the matter, and in finding out exactly what had happened and who was to blame.   She had, of course, explained to Nicholas that seeing that she had been left in a pretty dire situation, financially, it would be good if there was some kind of compensation from somebody since that would at least help her to keep the house.   If the transporter driver had been responsible, or if his company had failed to maintain their vehicle and/or the mechanism adequately, then perhaps she could at least take some kind of civil action against them.

Nicholas, naturally, understood this, since he had been only too acutely aware of the financial situation that Sandra would now find herself it.   Though he had not been aware of the minutiae of their day to day financial matters, he had known, particularly when Sandra sold the car, that all was not well.   It had been impossible, too, to ignore the piles of unopened mail that was always visible in the house – an indication that they were too afraid or disheartened to open letters because they knew without doing so what they were and what they would say.   There was no point in lecturing or debating this, since the person mostly responsible, his brother, was no longer there to either help or hinder, so to apportion blame now was irrelevant and futile.

"But what was the scooter for?"   he asked, in order to change the subject, he thought, slightly.

Sandra laughed and, almost embarrassed, said that she was going to track down the driver, but it was difficult to do that on public transport since he was not local and she would need to search around a bit.   She said she had managed to get the address from the police – she did not say she had done this by deception, and by, unwittingly, dropping WPC Curtis in to the mire, and possibly blighting her police career for ever   - and that if they were not going to prioritise it, then she would do something herself.

Nicholas was not one to let a good opportunity pass him by, and, ignoring the fact that before half an hour ago, she was persona non gratis within the family, asked why on earth she had not asked him to help. He had transport!   It would be better for him to go with her, because the man might be violent.   She had no idea what she might be getting herself into.   The driver would doubtless not wish to be held responsible … after all who would wish to be considered responsible for somebody's death?   No, it was not safe for her to go on her own, she must have been mad to even contemplate it.   Silly girl!   Silly girl!   What was she thinking!

Sandra did not know what to think!   On the one hand,

it would be really helpful to have the car ..... but not necessarily Nicholas!   She would probably feel better to have somebody with her ...... but not necessarily Nicholas!   It was nice to have somebody concerned about her welfare, and her safety ...... but not necessarily Nicholas!   There's another fine mess she had got herself into!

Sandra made appropriate noises and thanked him for his offer. She said she would need to chase up what the latest situation was with DS Daniels before she went gadding off and challenging the driver – with or without Nicholas's company, for which she was really ever so grateful.   She would definitely keep him 'in the picture' and as soon as she thought it was the right time to set off, she would 'give him a ring'.   She hoped that this did not sound too much like a brush off, since it was always possible that if things did not work out in any other way, she might just have to swallow her finer feelings and take him up on his offer.   She sincerely hoped not, but beggars cannot be choosers, now can they?

Nicholas did not seem to be in any great hurry to leave, and though it was quite nice to have somebody – anybody – to talk to face to face he would not have been her first choice, not even her 101 choice!   She was, though, fed up with only talking to friendly faces via Skype, and all other conversations were either domestic, as in good morning to the check out in the supermarket or 'Yes, I know I am in the red, and I am in the process of sorting it' to almost everybody else. That and the round the houses dialogue between her and the police, were the only human contact she had these days.   She made another cup of tea and as they sat chatting in almost an embarrassed fashion, with Nicholas hoping that the ice would thaw and Sandra aware that he could just as well been anybody, anybody at all, who was alive, present, and filling a gap in her lonely and increasingly crabby existence.   She knew she was permanently angry, and hostile, and reclusive, and ….... .   Beneath it all, she did understand that really she was sad, and isolated, and scared, and …. lots of other vulnerable emotions that she tried desperately to hide from the world by being really nasty and suspicious.   How would she ever have any friends again if she did not go back to being a half way pleasant human being.   She had been – hard as it was now to believe – fun and attractive and popular!   God, that was a long time ago!   What had ever happened to that person! She could not really blame Simon's death, it was creeping up on her long before that.   Simon had not been one for outings, or friendships, or joint ventures.   She had learned over time to be self-sufficient and to keep her head down and   'soldier on'. It had become an implacable outer coat that hid her more vulnerable and easily hurt side.   She had needed to build a fortress, not because Simon had been deliberately nasty, or, heaven forbid, violent!   We are not talking about domestic violence here, of any sort, but it was difficult to live in a vacuum, without anybody reminding you that you were not only there, but that people were glad you were there!   You could not expect that from your children – they really only knew what they had when they no longer had it – we were the same at their age – but it would not have been too much to ask from an adult, an intelligent and perfectly civilised adult at that.   But he was gone, and despite all, she missed him.   Warts and all!

As she contemplated all this she had absolutely no idea that Nicholas had been waffling on, and suddenly coming to, she realised that he was saying that he would be happy to do a bit of sorting around the house, take the dog out, mend things …. would that be helpful?   She could not help laughing, and said that she had been used to mending things and doing the 'sorting round the house' herself for a very long time, and the only exercise she seemed to be getting these days was taking the poor old dog out for a walk.   He really missed Simon, and had acted strangely for weeks afterwards.

Even Nicholas seemed to get the picture that he was barking up the wrong tree here, and was about to give up in defeat, whether to accept that he had lost the war, or merely the current battle, he was not sure, when Sandra suddenly said that if she decided at some time in the future to have a few days away, just to try and escape her surroundings, could he, would he, perhaps, be able to keep an eye on the dog and the house?   He saw this as at least an invitation to stay in touch, and was immediately rejuvenated almost as though she had said 'Why don't we both go away for a few days to escape our surroundings'!   Little acorns and all that!

He went off happier, and said, as she waved him off, 'I'll give you a ring, or call in in a day or two, to see if you have any more news?   Don't forget, my car, and myself are completely at your disposal, if you need to go anywhere.   But, Sandra, I really don't think you should go on your own …. God knows what you might be walking into!"

She knew that he was right really, and thought, after all, he's not such a bad old stick, is he!   Maybe she would be better off with a man's presence if she went off and confronted the driver.   She had never thought about it as 'confrontation' before, merely seeing it as a fact finding mission, but perhaps Nicholas was right. The man had a lot to lose, perhaps?   His job, certainly. If he was really negligent, then maybe even more, his freedom, perhaps?   It was hard to know what to think. She did not want to bring anybody's life crashing down, but whether by accident, design, or negligence, Simon's life had ended due to the Toyota Yaris crashing down, and there was nothing worse that could happen to a person, than that they should actually lose their life well before their three score years and ten.   Her sympathy had to be with Simon, not with this unknown man (or woman????) whatever remorse he or she was suffering now.

Chapter 10. *The mystery of the phone*

Early the next morning the telephone rang.   It was DS Daniels, none too pleased that she had been given the information by his naive young colleague, but not really able to lambaste Sandra as he would have liked to do. He knew that he himself would have done exactly as she had, and that had it been his wife, he would be jumping up and down and demanding that heads roll and gavels fall.

He had to mention the fact, simply because he wanted to let her know that he was aware, but he was not inclined to overstate the fact that WPC Curtis was carpeted for her naivete, because he did not want Sandra to get the impression (right though it was!) that the young constable had acted wrongly and that for some reason Sandra was not entitled to the information that she had managed to obtain.   It was a difficult juxtaposition for Daniels, sympathising with her from a personal viewpoint, but needing to toe the party line over the breach in confidentiality by his young colleague, as a member of the force.   Collective responsibility is a bugger sometimes!

He told her that they had spoken to the driver now, and had a bit of a clearer picture, but he was still very vague and was claiming amnesia about everything prior to finding himself in an ambulance.   Daniels had not realised, until they had really gone into the incident, that he had been taken to hospital too, because he had passed out at the scene, and even when he was brought round he was incoherent and dangerously agitated and confused.   He had been seen at A & E but had discharged himself later that evening and left without informing anybody.   How he had got home, he said, was a complete mystery!   If Daniels was dubious about this story, he expressed no such opinion to Sandra, but merely said that he could have been hit by something – obviously not as heavy as a car or he would have more than amnesia – and concussion was a really tricky thing to predict.   They were still 'on the case' and would keep her informed.   Sandra was less than comforted by any of this, and was even less delighted when he threw in, almost as a passing shot, that he had investigated the phone, and the driver definitely did not have the phone, and that it was impossible to say who had it at present.   He, the driver lived nowhere close to Lincolnshire, and there was nothing to make them believe that he had been anywhere near there in the recent past.   So it was still a mystery, but he would bear it in mind, though phones were a bit like umbrellas, bicycles and pens these days, misguidedly regarded as communal property by some. (So it was a man thought Sandra! That was a relief! She would not like to think of a woman being involved in it.   If it was her, she knew she would have made every effort to help the police, and even, she thought, though it was easy to say without being put to the test, that she might even have called on the 'widow' to express some kind of sorrow, or at least some kind of mitigation).   Daniels continued, since it had been switched off, or more likely if it had been merely 'lost' rather than nicked, it would just have run out of battery.   After all, it could reasonably have lain in the gutter or on the grass at the scene of the accident and been picked up by anyone passing between the time of the incident and now, or not!   Phones got stolen, lost, mislaid all the time – once again he threw in the opt out clause that it was one of the most common crimes, etc. etc. etc.   Sandra did not like to tell him that she had scoured every blade of grass, every pile of dog dirt, every nook and cranny almost immediately after that fateful day.   She could not, of course, say for certain that it had not 'gone' from that spot overnight, but certainly as of the following morning, if there was a phone to be found, she would have found it!

When the call had ended, Sandra was surer than ever that left to their own devices nothing would really be done.   She believed that Daniels probably meant well, and he was not unsympathetic, but it certainly was not at the top of the pile.   If they did anything at all, it would be piecemeal and when they had a minute to spare.   Like mobile phones, Simon was also an unimportant commodity!   Sod them.   She would do something herself.

Sandra had a poor night's sleep again, and as her body thrashed around trying to get comfortable, so her mind careered around all the possibilities, the likelihoods, the 'what ifs'. She had been troubled by a wisp of thought that kept flitting tantalisingly close to the periphery of her mind, and then wafting off again. She just knew it was important, but had no idea what it was …. After a very long time, not long before the sun was due to rise, she finally fell into a kind of half sleep. She rarely remembered her dreams, but since she had probably been at the very least semi-conscious this time, when she awoke, feeling a bit better and a little bit more rested, she found she had still kept hold of the last remnants of her dream..... Simon's jacket! That was what she had been trying to bring to the front of her mind. She had not registered the importance at the time, but she now knew that the newish jacket that she had last seen Simon wearing before he left the house with Stef was hanging in the garage. Stef had said that he had changed his jacket and put on an old moth-eaten one. Goodness knows why he would have just left it hanging there in the garage instead of in the house, but who cares why...... that must be where the ticket was!   Hoo bloody Rah!   Though she was alone, in a mad kind of way, she looked around to see if anybody had heard her exclaim!   Guilt was a dreadful thing and plagued us even when there was nobody else to witness our sins.   Well, she knew she had given up the search – or more accurately put it into its rightful place on the runner up podium in her order of priority – but that did not mean she had to abandon all hope that it would ever be found, now did it?

As soon as she got up and had put on a dressing gown and slippers, she forced herself to make a cup of coffee, feed the dog, pull the curtains, plump up the cushions and put away last night's washing up, all in order to prove to herself that she was not prioritising the lottery over her feelings for Simon.   Also, she had to admit that having been disappointed many times before, she was fearful lest this should be yet another wild goose chase.   Finally though she plucked up the courage and walking through the adjoining door into the garage, she felt inside the coat pockets and there in the left hand one, nestling, ….. oh my Lord, …   was a piece of paper …...   Oh, (the disappointment was almost palpable and her whole demeanour seemed to slump and shrink) ... not a ticket, just a piece of paper with numbers on it.   She had recalled what Simon had said 'I have the numbers here, look here they are', and had interpreted that in her mind over the weeks as meaning he had circled the numbers of the actual ticket.   Oh bloomin norah! Did that mean that she had been searching for a piece of paper which was of absolutely no consequence all this time.   She could hardly phone Camelot and say these were our numbers because my husband wrote them down on a piece of paper the evening he died.   They might not laugh, out of respect for the dead, but they would certainly not say, 'Oh well here you are then here are your winnings. Congratulations!   Have a wonderful, debt free, worry free life!"

So, all that had been in vain.   Neither the transporter driver, nor the ambulance personnel, nor the nursing staff at A & E, nor the Co-op Funeral Care people

…..none of them, not even a lucky passer by, had purloined the ticket, because the ticket had not existed….. well it might have once existed, but she knew now that she had never seen Simon with it in his hand, and knowing his absent mindedness over such matters, he might easily have forgotten to actually buy the ticket, and even if he did, then the chances of him keeping it safe were even less certain.   It could be anywhere now, or nowhere!

Oh well.   That was it.   It was a nice dream while it lasted.   Back to reality.   She could not make up her mind whether this meant it was more imperative to go and track down the driver, or less important.   She could pursue the search for justice for Simon just as easily by sitting on the backs of those people paid to do such things, namely DS Daniels and his colleagues. She would have to torment them and sit on them and drive them and make herself a proper nuisance, but she could do that, of course she could, she was just in that frame of mine.   Sitting on them would be no problem.   A positive pleasure, in actual fact!   She was just in the mood to do exactly that!

She had no choice now, she had to push ahead and be positive.   She kept reminding herself that things were no different now than they would have been previously. The debts (with the exception of the dreaded Co-operative Funeral Services which was of course a new and unsolicited debt), were familiar to her so why was she feeling so destroyed by them now?   She had lived with the self-preserving attitude of 'don't let the buggers grind you down' for a very long time, single handedly.   Nothing had changed.   She just had to pretend that Simon was working away, silently, single-mindedly, in the other room.   But something had changed.   She had lost something.   She had somehow been dealt a near fatal blow, but she was now determined that 'near fatal' was not 'fatal', not like the blow that had befallen Simon.   That had been truly fatal.   She now knew she had to press on and make somebody pay.   Both financially and physically. That would not only solve the practical problems and pay the bills, but it would also solve her more emotional problems.   She did not like to even contemplate the word 'vengeance' but she knew that she would FEEL better if she had done everything she could to understand what had happened, why, and who and how …. Not much to ask, was it, to explain how a man went out one evening to walk a dog and never came home again.

So, back to logistics!   Selling the house now was, she knew, not an 'if' but a   'when'.   But that would obviously take time.   You just did not take it down to the 'house dealership' and sell it on, or trade it in!   The worry was CFC.   She was not sure how long they would wait before getting really pushy, like all of her other creditors, for their money.   She could not blame them. Here was she planning to to join the rest of those 'chasing payment' by pursuing her 'rights' by way of the transporter driver's insurers.

So needs must, and all that ….. what a girl had to do, a girl had to do.   Another cup of coffee, then, while she planned her strategy and her focus..... DS Daniels, his superiors?   Her MP?   Her local councillors?   The 'owners' of the transport company .... whoever they were?   The political machinery would come in very useful, she thought!   Perhaps it was not necessary to do all the work herself.   She made her list.   It was not long, but it was influential and could be very effective, she thought.   She wondered how many of these played golf with the Chief Constable?   Just a thought. Who did she know that was on the local newspaper?

Sandra knew that the best way to get information 'out there' was by Social Media, but not being an aficionado of any of these methods, she had to stick to the old fashioned means.   She remembered that one of Amber's old boy friends had been a trainee journalist on the local paper, and she started off by skyping Amber to refresh her memory.   She thought he was called Kyle Jennings, but she was not sure, that might have been the punk with the tattoos and the piercings. She needed to not make that mistake!   Amber said that she would contact Ryan Marriott (not Kyle

Jennings who was the apprentice plumber, nor Wayne Atherton, who was the punk with the tats!) because she could do it via facebook which would be quicker and better. They could perhaps get the whole injustice 'trending' …. whatever that was, thought Sandra, which according to Amber would be just 'awesome'.

After what seemed like a very short time, probably only just over the week, the story seemed to have become widespread and DS Daniels was being pushed by his bosses to let then know what all this furore was about, and what they had, or not, as the case may be, done about it.   He had tried to deflect the implied criticism by explaining that it might not even be a police matter, but that did not have anything like the desired effect. As far as the 'powers that be' were concerned, it just as easily might be a police matter, and how had it taken him so long to know one way or the other.   What had he been doing for all these weeks/months?   Too little effort!   Too little consideration for the way it looked!   What had he been thinking!   Why had he not told them that there was this potential banana skin!

New enquiries were launched.   New avenues explored. It was a very bizarre sort of 'accident'.   Could it have been something else?   What did they know about Simon Jameson?   Was he known to the police? Anything on file? Any links with terrorist organisations? Had he any previous links with the transporter driver? Why had the transporter driver not been 'properly' brought in for questioning?   Who decided that he was telling the truth when he claimed to have amnesia? What kind of excuse was that?   Sounded dubious to say the least!   Did Simon Jameson have enemies? Was it gang or drug related?   Could it have been a reprisal or a revenge killing?   Indeed the whole of the top brass seemed to suddenly become obsessed with being kept 'in the loop' and questions were asked by Councillors or MPs, and MPs raised questions with Ministers, and no end of sabre rattling was heard around the higher echelons of power!   Sandra suddenly knew how right people were in talking about the power of 'Social Media'.   She would never look on it as another craze like the yo-yo or the Rubik cube

131

again!

The local paper, courtesy of Ryan Marriott who was more than grateful in these early stages of his career to receive pats on the back and even a bonus for his part in 'launching' the campaign to get 'justice for Simon Jameson'.

One of the most welcome aspects of the publicity was the receipt of a letter from the Managing Director of the Benevolent and Compassionate Funeral Services to tell Sandra that she was not to worry about the account.   The company was fully aware of the circumstances and would not pursue the debt until such time as she found herself in a position to settle. They felt her loss, and commiserated with her in her misfortune .... etc. etc. etc.

She did not know whether to laugh or to cry.   She was delighted to know that the threatening letters would stop, for the time being, but was saddened that it took the full weight of the press, the politicians, social media and public opinion to make companies realise that they were not being baulked for their money out of pure obstinacy and because people were profligate and feckless, but that sometimes people had circumstances and situations which made them vulnerable and needy.

Chapter 11:   *A Stranger at the Door*

About a week after the letter from the undertakers, Sandra made a decision. A decision which had nothing now to do with debts (although she still had those!) but because she suddenly felt the need for a new start, a new life.   She had a look in Yellow Pages and picked out at random an estate agent and rang them to ask that they advise her about putting her house on the market.   James Crossman, who picked up the call, made an arrangement to call on her the next morning at 10.30, to take some details and start the ball rolling. Sandra felt glad that she had taken this step, and suddenly realised just how much she had begun to hate the house, the neighbourhood, the lifestyle .... everything about the place. She knew that if she did not make a complete change she would end up hating herself, and would turn into a real misery, blighting not only her own life, but her daughters' lives too. She did not have to live like this. She might not make anything selling the house, since the outstanding mortgage was big, plus the arrears, but at least she could start afresh and there would be enough to at least pay the main creditors. After all, she was on her own now. She could live anywhere, do anything. The world could be her oyster! The not quite remodelled Sandra found that she could not stop herself adding .... 'without a hidden pearl though, I dare say!'

The rest of the day she cleaned, polished, scrubbed, tried to tidy the garden, baked bread, bought flowers and put these in vases strategically around the house. She knew that James Crossman would not be taking much of this into consideration, but she was glad to give herself a proper reason to be busy and constructive.

She had spoken to the girls on Skype and had been disconcerted by their less than favourable reaction to her decision to sell the house.   They were concerned, she knew, that they would no longer have their 'base' to return to, and also that this was not a good time for her to be making momentous decisions of that sort. The investigation into the accident was still on-going and they could not understand why now! She was walking a bit of a tightrope.   She did not want to sound as though she was euphoric that now she had just herself to consider, and that all her encumbrances were 'off her hands', but neither did she want them to feel that she was suffering from 'empty nest syndrome' coupled with the horrors of losing their father so suddenly and that they were expected to return home to assuage her loneliness and isolation.   Whichever side of the tightrope she fell would be misconstrued by her volatile and newly grown daughters.   She knew only too well that they were at that strange time of adulthood when they wanted to be both grown ups and children.   They wanted the security of a place and a mother to run to when the going got rough, at the same time as demanding and welcoming their long anticipated freedom.   But they also wanted to be 'doing the right thing' as adults should, caring for their poor mother in her hour of need, but not being mature enough to anticipate and understand that she too might appreciate her own independence and freedom, now that it was at last available to her.   Their opinions mattered, of course they did, but she would go ahead because once she was settled somewhere else, they would once again have their base, and they would see that she was perfectly capable of looking after herself and was not in need of their watch-dogging! Cruel to be kind.   It would all come out in the wash ….. all those clichés might be trite, but they were none the less useful and true!

So the next morning, she was up bright and breezy, ready for the visit from James Crossman, with the house as respectable and pristine as it was going to be after five years of scrimping and saving over decorating and repairs.   Still, she would just have to see what he said.   As long as it paid off the mortgage and the bills, she would be content to start again with a clean slate.

At a quarter to ten, there was a knock on the door and Sandra was very surprised because he was not just a bit early, but a whole 45 minutes early.   Was that eagerness or a bad memory.   Anyway, what did it matter.   She was ready for the visit anyway, so better early than late, she supposed.   Get it over and done with.

When she opened the door she was taken aback.   She would never have put the name and occupation to the face and apparel standing on the doorstep.   She was just going to say 'Good morning' you must be Mr. Crossman, when the young chap standing in front of her, without saying anything,   thrust a mobile phone into her hand and muttered a few incomprehensible words before standing in silence with Sandra just as open mouthed and for once speechless.   Eventually, she looked down at the phone, and recognised immediately that it was Simon's, which brought her back to her senses and she was just able to grab at the man's sleeve as he turned to walk away down the path. She was not sure whether grabbing at him was a good move or not.   He might lash out at her if she tried to stop him from leaving.   After all she had absolutely no idea who he was – he might be a homicidal maniac for all she knew!   He looked though more pathetic and browbeaten than dangerous, but looks can be deceiving.   Sandra's curiosity overcame her fear and she gently pulled his sleeve and urged him inside the house.   He went inside the house without any real struggle or reluctance, but certainly the 'insistence' was definitely more on her side than on his.

Once he was inside, she urged him to sit down.   By sign language she asked if he would like a cup of tea, and almost despite himself he had to smile, fleetingly, but smile he did.   She realised that what he had smiled at was the English propensity for offering   'a nice cup of tea' however bizarre or horrible the circumstances, and she broke the ice by laughing in response.

She asked who he was, and how he had got hold of the phone, but it was obvious that his English was virtually non-existent.   It was going to be a bit of a challenge to carry on a conversation, let alone get any real information from him.

He looked at her and finally took from his jacket pocket a folded up piece of paper, which he handed to her. She took it gingerly, though why she eyed it so suspiciously even she could not say.   Having held it in her hand for a few moments without doing anything with it, the man seemed to get more anxious that she should read it, and gestured at the paper and muttered again, so that whatever the language, his desire that she should open the paper was perfectly evident.   She did as she was told.

The page was virtually full of very neat, very precise

writing.   It was in English, but seemed to be English that had been directly translated from some other language, with obviously wrong vocabulary in some places, though the gist of the story was very clear.

Dear Madam,

It read: My name is Abshir Daud.   I am an engineering student from Somalia.   I do not talk good English, so this missive is through my friend.

I sorry to keep the phone.   My friend tell me about your sorrow and I return.

I see your man when he hurt, but not know he was gone.

I must be to England to find a sister.   She leave since May a year gone and we hear nothing.   I find route to France, pay much money.   I speak with man who I see smoking near ship.   I know his face from other who spoke before, but had not money for him.   I sent by father for sister, so have more to pay. Father has good business in Djibouti and can afford but sadly before in 2008 I visit UK.   I say to study, but not leave UK or study proper and find working so sent back and not allow again to England official.

Man say he all the time drives cars from France to England and will take.   I have to hide in car on top of big lorry and be very still.   It not bad.   It not so far.   I give him money, and he do as he say.   All go easy.

He load car, lot of cars, but when we are over he keep going.   He not stay still so I can come off.   I stuck in car on top of truck.   He say he forget.   I not know if it so.   We get to this town.   He meet with somebody where your man hurt.   Some important man, I think. They shout at one another.   He climb up, I saw, before he let me out of car and before other angry man come along, he get parcel from underneath wheel on one other car.   Drugs, maybe but I not sure, but think so. He give to angry man.   He let me down after shouting man gone, but just move truck round corner.   I ask how I go forward.   I am stuck here.   I do not know where it is.   I have given him my money and I am afraid.   He said I should …. 'fuck off'..   I said where to.   He say 'I don't give a fuck' and he climbed into truck to sleep.   I sat on the ground.   I was not good. I tired.   I crying.   I lost.

Then along come man with dog.   I hear, and he too hear noise from the cars on top.   I think man not fix properly.   I lucky I not fallen off on all way from dock to here!

When man with dog come, and cars move.   He go tap on driver's window to say cars move.   Man not happy. He get out with big metal thing …. a metal tool.   He follow man to back of truck, but the car then make bigger noise and begin fall and miss driver man, but hit man with dog. The dog ran away.   Driver was frighted. He went this way and that way.   He put head in hands. He lit cigarette.   Very not happy.   Talking to self and cursing.   He got out his phone,   but put back.   Found your man phone and phone people.   He threw phone into bushes.   I find.   I sorry I keep so long.   I see lights flashing and the cars of the police coming near so I went quick away.   I not wish to be found before I find sister.   I find now she lost to us.

Please excuse me.   I not mean harm and am regretful for your man and for my fear which cause you more trouble.

Abshir Daud

It was difficult for Sandra to have a conversation with Abshir, much as she would have really liked to.   There was so many questions, so much to ask him.   She asked, now, having learned her lesson about the tea, whether he would like water, or something to eat, but he stood up immediately, bowed very seriously, shaking his head and saying what sounded like 'wonky summer key'.   With that he was gone.   He almost ran out of the house and when she reached to door he was being picked up by an old M registered Ford Mondeo. She had not seen one like that for years.

When she returned inside the house, Sandra did a bit of research on Google, she found the phrase "waan ka xumakay" which was just translated as 'Sorry'. That might be the wonkey summer key, and it would make sense, given the sentiments at the end of the letter. Well where did that all leave her?

After a lot of thought, she decided that she had only one real option. She needed to tell DS Daniels about the visit from Abshir Daud and show him the letter. She wondered who the 'angry man' was that Abshir had thought was important. He had, apparently taken the drugs, so it was perhaps sensible to assume that Mr. Car Transporter worked for him, rather than the other way around. Could it be that, as a sideline, Mr. Car Transporter ran his people smuggling enterprise, possibly unknown to Mr. Important? She wondered what the row was about. She was never likely to know, but that did not stop her speculating.

She rang the police station, either by accident or

design, giving Abshir time to be well gone out of the area before Daniels knew anything about it.   She had no intention of doing anything other than telling the police about the visit and the letter, and the implications of what the letter contained, but she was reluctant to be responsible for Abshir being picked up as a direct result of her actions.

DS Daniels was not on duty, and was not expected back for two more days.   This was a blow since Sandra was not content to let that much time elapse, but she was equally not relishing the thought of telling some new, sceptical, disinterested and unfriendly police personage either.   DS Daniels was not exactly 'friendly', and there was something she found two faced about him, though this was a view based, she fully appreciated, on absolutely nothing at all, just 'intuition'.   But he was not new to the 'case' and so she didn't have to go over old ground endlessly again. He had got, she thought, less sceptical, but perhaps more wary, though that was good old Mrs. Intuition again, and he seemed to have got more and more interested.   She was in two minds.   She decided to let it lie for the time being and then perhaps she would write it all up for Daniels, make a copy of the 'letter' and take it into the station herself in a couple of days or so.   If he was there, fine, if not, she would have to talk to somebody else.   She could not leave it too long or it would look badly for her, as though she was hiding something or there was something fishy going on, and the last thing she wanted, or needed, was for some clever insurance investigator somewhere to decide that something was dodgy.   The more she thought about it, the less comfortable she got with sitting on the letter, and not giving it to the police.   Perhaps, in any case, she should speak to somebody else.   She only had Daniels word that he was doing anything at all, and look how cheesed off he had been because she had spoken to the other one, WPC Curtis.   No point talking to her again though, she'd be terrified now to put her head above the parapet!   Let it lie for now, but before the end of the day she'd have to make a decision.

She had forgotten totally about James Crossman, so

146

when the knock came to the door, her first instinct was that the Somalian had returned. She rushed to the door but this time there was no mistaking the fact that the man standing on her doorstep was an estate agent, but older than she had pictured him. She thought of estate agents these days as young, trendy, gobby and full of themselves. This man was certainly gobby, but he was probably about 60. Certainly neat and dapper, but definitely not 'trendy'. Old school. Almost certainly the 'boss' – one man band, possible? It was a woman she had spoken to when she rang, and she had implied that 'she would see who might be free'. A ruse Sandra now suspected! The woman had seemed to forget that little embellishment when she had gone on to immediately confirm the 10.30 appointment with 'our Mr. Crossman'. Wife? Possibly? As for full of himself, that was most certainly true, despite his age. 'So sharp he could cut himself', as her mother would have said! Just as she had pictured him.

"Hello, Mrs. Jameson, I'm James Crossman. You spoke to my secretary yesterday I gather. Want to put the house on the market, is that it?"

He left her no time to answer or respond to this brusque introduction in any way, but as he sailed past her he said "Now, my dear, will Mr. Jameson be joining us?   I always prefer to speak to the house owners together, saves any unfortunate misunderstandings on anybody's part, doesn't it, eh?"

He did not even listen to her reply.   He walked in, almost visibly grimacing with the disappointment that this house most certainly did not measure up to the one next door which they had had on their books recently.   Unfortunately that one was not exclusive to them because the vendors wanted a quick move, and one of their competitors had been quicker off the mark and hence got the sale and the commission.   No this one was nothing like that one.   No comparison. Still, his face said, some are diamonds, some are glass, but if we can pass off glass for diamonds, well that only proves how bloody brilliant we are.   He obviously knew he could sell skis to the Arabs, and bikinis to the Eskimos!

She was not at all taken with him. Her mind was elsewhere, and yesterday's firm resolve to sell the house had dimmed, so she said without any real enthusiasm 'You'd probably prefer to just wander round and have a good look yourself – you don't need me under your feet, do you?"

In total contrast to her last visitor, James Crossman was blessed with the gift of the gab and replied that he would be happy to do that so long as she had the kettle on and a nice cup of tea and perhaps a slice of cake waiting when he had finished. They could then have a bit of a chat, and Mr. Jameson could join them and he – well they - could sign on the dotted line. In case she had been too thick to understand his two previous references to 'Mr. Jameson' (given that she had not responded in any way) he once again threw in the explanation that he preferred to have the 'man of the house' 'in on the act'.   This prevented time wasting and disagreements down the line, it being a bit of a complicated business sometimes with big decisions to be made.   Better be safe than sorry, Sandra, he said, patting her on the shoulder.   His growing list of calumnies was seriously compounded by calling her 'Sandra'! Though normally she would not mind this, indeed most times she would prefer it, but from him she found it over familiar, demeaning and definitely unwelcome.

We'll have to see about that! thought Sandra.   There will be no tea or cake for you, James, my good man!

She could hear him stamping on floorboards and pacing out rooms, and far from hoping that he would find everything satisfactory, for some unfathomable reason Sandra found herself wishing she had not spent all of yesterday cleaning and preparing.   He would have found fault, and looked down his nose at everything in any case and at least then there would have been some real justification, now she just knew he would be less than flattering about the place, simply because it was his nature to be so.

When he had finished looking around, he walked into the kitchen in full anticipation that he would be greeted, as he had requested, with tea and cake, but poor Mr. Jameson was destined to be disappointed. Such a pity she had not made any cake this week, such a lot of calories! (or any week, come to that!) such a lot of calories!   Biscuits?   They had not been found in her cupboard since ….. well for a very long time. Just indulgences and full of sugar and calories.   She knew Mr. Crossman would understand, being an elderly gentleman, that these times people were much too over-indulgent!   He had asked for tea?   She was sure he would understand perfectly, being a man of the world, that since she was Mormon her religion forbade stimulants there was nothing like tea or coffee on the premises.   Just in case he thought her inhospitable, she should say also that they did not allow cola, or anything like that, but would he like a nice fresh glass of water .... it was filtered and very refreshing.   No, they could not have She wished she could offer him milk, but unfortunately, though obviously Mormons were allowed milk – of course they were – she herself was lactose intolerant, so there was no milk in the house either.   Mr. Cross declined the water and edged towards the dining table fishing out from his brief case the forms for her to sign.   He did not like this woman, and the house was not up to much, but business was business, and not every oyster could contain a pearl!

But before he got there and sat down, probably in his discomfiture, he dug the hole deeper.   He unfortunately waffled on, and on, and on ....   Having listened to his 'providing you do this', and 'providing you don't do that' and 'providing you do not harbour exaggerated expectations over price' and 'providing you let us, as the experts, advise you and do as we say' Sandra had quickly decided that she and James Crossman were never likely to get along.   He additionally blotted his copy book by eulogising about the fantastic décor and impeccable taste of the house that had just been sold next door: such exquisite taste, so beautifully maintained.   You could eat your food off of the floor, apparently!   (Probably because that bitch Terri never cooked and they did not need to get anything dirty because they permanently lived on takeaways and with takeaways you just chuck the debris into the dustbin, thought Sandra cattily.)   She was extremely anxious therefore to let him know that neither would he be indulged with regard to this other request, namely that she should 'sign on the dotted line'.   She took great pleasure in telling him that she would have to think things over more carefully.   In light of his advice that the house was not in as good a state of décor or upkeep as his firm preferred, and since it was a very complicated exercise to sell a house, as a naive and poorly educated little woman she had better think again.   So, no,   she would certainly not be signing his exclusive commission option, or any other option, at the moment, and almost certainly, never!

She added, as she patted his shoulder and urged him towards the door, that in response to his request that

Mr. Jameson join them,   unfortunately Mr. Crossman was much too late for that!   Indeed they were all late. Mr. Jameson was late – because he was now 'the late Mr. Simon Jameson, RIP' and Mr. James Crossman was therefore too late to demand his presence at the discussions.   He was very much 'too late' to get a signature from the 'man of the house', and he should have been content with that of 'the woman of the house', namely **Mrs. Jameson, not Sandra,** who has ever right, alone, without any hand holding, without any guidance or approval to sell the bloody house!

James Crossman left the house feeling mystified as to why she had been so hostile.   He could only put it down to her relatively recent bereavement.   Yes, he had to admit that it had been a bit of a faux pas on his part mentioning the husband, but he only did that in passing.   She did not have to take it so ill!   Could she not have just said she was a widow?   Was that so difficult?   Ah well, we all have bad days.   Move on! That was all he could do.   The house was a bit of a disappointment anyway.   Not missed out too much on that one he thought.   Not much commission, and a lot of hard selling needed.   If you added in the touchiness of Sandra Jameson, then whoever took it on would certainly earn their pittance.   No, he was well out of that one.   Lucky escape.

Chapter 12:   *Making a discovery*

Sandra had to laugh to herself at the look on James Crossman's face as he wandered off down the pathway.   Pompous old codger!

She went back into the kitchen, and for the first time really looked at poor Simon's mobile phone which she had put down on the work surface when she answered the door to Mr. Pompous.   It was obviously dead as a dodo.   The battery had long since run out and whoever recharged it now would probably have to re-enter the password.   Unlike her, Simon had been a bit of a stickler for passwords: that would be a bit of a puzzle in itself.   With Simon's technical mind, it could be like cracking the bloody enigma code. Who did she know that had worked at Bletchley Park!   Anyway, she'd give it a go!   Nothing to lose.   She needed to plug it in first of all to recharge it. She could do nothing with it until it had some life in it.   Let it charge away, it was not going anywhere, now that it was back home!

Her thoughts turned to Abshir Daud. He seemed like a nice, gentle soul and the bit in the letter that said that his sister was lost to them was really said.   Had he meant she was actually dead, or that she had somehow made herself too alienated from her family to ever be welcomed back?   If the latter she so wanted to say to Abshir – and probably more to his father – not to discard her irrespective of what she had done – you could never say sorry, or forgive somebody, or tell them you love them, once they were gone for good. Death was very final and it was horrible to be left with regrets and 'if onlys'.   She knew only too well how that felt.

She felt the need to get out of the house.   The aftermath of Mr. Crossman still permeated the place, the phone was useless until it was charged, she had scoured and scrubbed the place yesterday so there was no real housework to be done, despite Mr. Crossman's withering glances!

She went over to the kitchen miscellaneous drawer and took out once again 'the letter'. She was not a religious person, and not given to touchy feely mumbo jumbo, but she found herself just in her thoughts, asking Simon what she should do. It was no surprise to her that she did not hear voices or get some kind of inspiration from beyond the grave, but after a few moments she definitely felt clearer in her own mind what she was going to do. She would go to the police station, and she would speak to somebody higher up than DS Daniels. She knew that by this time there would have been a lot of agitation within the corridors or power over the hype in social media and the press, so maybe she would be taken seriously this time, and it was not as though she did not have something more to contribute – she had Abshir's words, and an eye witness account of what had happened. All right, it did sound as though it was an accident, rather than anything actually malicious, but there was negligence, surely, and there was the possible drug connection. She tried not to think about the people smuggling aspect, since she did not like to think of anybody

helping Abshir in his search for his sister as 'unlawful'.
She did realise that he was just one of many
thousands, and that people like the transporter driver
were making millions, out of the suffering of these poor
souls, and many of them ended up criminalised and
even enslaved.   No, despite her sympathy with Abshir,
she had no doubt whatsoever how she felt about those
that trafficked and made huge amounts of blood
money out of the suffering of others.

When she arrived at the police station, her 'friend'
Sergeant Pickles was in his usual spot behind the desk.
There were a handful of people already hovering
around, and a lot of activity both sides of the glass
divide.   Despite dealing with a 'customer' and the fact
that there were several other people waiting, Sergeant
Pickles saw her enter, and immediately said to the
person he was dealing with, 'just one moment, I shan't
be long....' and without leaving the office, took a couple
of steps across to the opening into the inner sanctum
and called across to somebody to 'tell them upstairs
that Mrs. Jameson is here'.   To her he said, 'Take a

seat, if you can, they won't be long …. they're on their way'.   Sandra had no idea who 'they' were, or why they were 'on their way', and since there were no seats available, she just continued to hover and await the arrival of 'they'.

After a very short while, and much to the consternation of most of the ever growing and patiently waiting crowd, she was ushered into the 'inner sanctum'.   She found herself in a small room – on television it would be called 'an interview room', but since the person leading her was anxious that she not feel intimidated or alarmed, he just said 'let's just go into here, it's quieter and I can hear myself think – it's chaos out there!'

He introduced himself as Detective Inspector Riley (my how she was going up the ranks!) and he apologised for what must seem like very slow progress in investigating the horrible event.   He thought he should

160

explain that they had run into one or two problems along the way – had DS Daniels explained?　No, oh well you must think that we are very, very slow then! He obviously was walking a tightrope between trying to be lightweight and non-intimidating, and at the same time remembering that to her it was definitely not a lightweight matter.　Simon Jameson was dead. Whatever of their other challenges around the whole case, they were all irrelevant to the widow.　So, for all kinds of reasons, some of which he was extremely reluctant to divulge to Sandra, he was treading on egg shells.

He decided that there was a need to at least tell her that the transporter driver (now identified as Karl Kirs. The family was originally Estonian, he said, but Karl was born in the UK, and his grandfather had arrived in the UK directly after WWII and had met and married a Lithuanian woman refugee in 1952.　He was not sure why he was going into such detail.　He could only reluctantly admit to himself that he was putting off arriving at the point where he told her that Karl Kirs had disappeared off the face of the globe.　No notion why. The accident seemed negligent, but not criminal. They could understand that he might have been upset by it, but his disappearance was, apparently, out of character. He was known locally as cocky and aggressive and not one to run. Definitely not when, as far as they could see, there was nothing to run from.

Sandra let the DI tell his story; she did not interrupt, or ask anything. He was forced to fill the silence by explaining that they had discovered that Karl Kirs was something of an entrepreneur (Sandra could vouch for that!) and he had realised that cars were cheaper bought on the continent, particularly in the country in which they were manufactured. His father already had a haulage business for the past 22 years, and ran a fleet of lorries criss-crossing the Continent particularly into countries in the former Soviet bloc. He employed mainly men, some women, but mainly men because it can be a bit of a hairy business, and there have been hijacks and assaults from time to time, from within the Eastern European community living in the UK. They spoke the right languages and understood the culture, and in any case he felt more comfortable employing his own. Anyway, that was the father! Karl, though, had ideas of his own. He borrowed money from Kirs Senior and bought a second hand car transporter. He would travel across to Italy for Fiat, France for the Toyota, etc. and bring these back and sell on for a profit. His father was surprised, apparently, that he was doing very well and money was rolling in. He had paid back the loan in next to no time. This was the first setback that he had suffered, and that is why his father is genuinely puzzled why he would clear off like that. Nobody apparently knows where he has gone to. The transporter is still parked in his father's compound. Incidentally the local officers have called in experts to check the mechanism on the transporter and it is definitely faulty, but it looks like some kind of design fault which becomes more obvious coupled with wear and tear. Matter of time, apparently, though the insurance company (you will be pleased to know) are not challenging it on the grounds that it was not criminally negligent to be unaware of the deterioration. So, negligence definitely, and the family is, of course, very sorry that such a thing should happen, and will pay whatever compensation is asked of them, both through their insurance and from their own resources if necessary, so from Karl's point of view there would be no need to run. We are puzzled too.

Sandra took the letter out of her bag and had it on the table, face down, with her hand resting on it. DI Riley looked at it quizzically, but she said nothing. He then asked her outright if she was aware that DS Daniels had gone up to Derbyshire to make personal enquiries of the Kirs family on her behalf. When asked a direct question, of course, Sandra was required to answer that she had no idea that he had gone anywhere, or indeed done anything, on her behalf. He had seemed somewhat disinterested and even critical of her having gone via WPC Curtis to find out details of the driver's location. He had not come back to her with regard to information about the mobile phone, and all he had said was that the last known location of the mobile phone was nowhere close to the location of the driver, so he could not have had it.   It must have been picked up at the scene.   He was dismissive of its loss, and its significance, saying that phones were like umbrellas, bicycles and pens, everybody thought they were communal property!   She must have sounded quite critical of Daniels – more critical than she had believed herself to be.   All the time she had thought that perhaps she was the one that was wrong; was expecting too much.   After all it was not a 'crime' as such, so why should the police involve themselves in it? She told DI Riley that, yes, she had got the Derbyshire address from WPC Curtis, and had been intending to go and talk to them direct, about their insurance, since she had no life insurance on her husband and she was in severe financial difficulties,   but other circumstances had intervened.

Finally, she turned over the piece of paper under her hand, and handed it to DI Riley.   He looked puzzled, but read on until he came to the end.   As he read, he began to realise what it was and how important it was. It also realised that if Karl Kirs had 'other irons in the fire' and transporting cars was not his only, or even his main, occupation, that might explain his absence.

With this information, and the knowledge, rife within the station, that somebody else had also gone missing, he was beginning to put two and two together, and hopefully not make five!

He did not explain any of these latter thoughts to Sandra – they were merely a police matter, and only peripherally connected with the death of Simon Jameson.

Sandra explained about Abshir Daud and his visit to her. She did not say that she had delayed coming to the station because of Abshir, but did say that she had tried to contact DS Daniels and had been told that he was away for a couple of days. She had thought about waiting until he returned, since he had been the only person at the police station (apart from Sergeant Pickles and WPC Curtis) who she had even vaguely discussed it with and since she had got WPC Curtis into trouble the last time with DS Daniels, and since Sergeant Pickles had been a bit cross with her last time for making a fuss over nothing, she had decided to await DS Daniels return.   She had no idea what had changed her mind.   It simply was a desire to be doing something.

DI Riley told her that though the case was now officially closed in its own right, obviously it had tangential links to other possible on-going matters.   He assured her that she would be hearing from the Kirs' insurance company very swiftly.   As far as 'the other business' was concerned, they would definitely be looking into that, and may need her to help them in due course, if they managed to put a case together.   He was not at liberty to say, but there were issues behind the scenes which would significantly affect the pursuance, the time-scale and the likely outcome of these matters, and so for the moment at least he was grateful for her assistance and her patience.

As she was leaving, she asked him to thank DS Daniels on her behalf for his involvement and to apologise to him for sometimes being less than grateful.   He gave her a very funny look and an even stranger reply.   He said, I will certainly speak with him about all these matters as soon as he is available.   I will pass on your words and your thanks.   She was shown out, this time saying a genuine cheerio to Sergeant Pickles on her way past him.   He still had a foyer full of people queueing up awaiting his attention.

When she got home, she had something to eat, Skyped the girls to tell them the news about the insurance company agreeing to pay compensation.   Amber, always the shrewd one, told her that nothing was sure until she had that in writing and not to let them palm her off either with delaying tactics or a pittance.   She was not to accept anything, do anything,   say anything until she had spoken to her first.   Yes, Mum, said Sandra, and they all laughed.   She remembered then to pick their brains over Simon's possible passwords for his phone.   Neither of the girls had any clear idea what it was, but promised to think about it and ring her. Something electronic, probably?   Wouldn't be anything normal, like other people use family names, or birthdays.   He was not built like that.   He would not even have remembered their birthdays – he hardly remembered their names most of the time.   She chided them for being so unkind, but all of the rebukes were said lovingly and with fond memories.

Sandra felt better than she had done for many days. She still had a big pile of unpaid bills, she still had no husband, she had a feeble message left on the answer phone by Nicholas bleating that she had not called him, but she still felt better despite no tangible change in her circumstances.

Then she thought she would have a go with the phone. She looked around at Simon's things – his tools, his books, his gadgets.   She had not had the heart or enthusiasm to store them away and his workspace was just as he left it – no wonder Mr. Pompous Crossman had turned his nose up.   She laughed at the memory of his face as he left.   Texas Instruments? Transistor? Software? Circuit?   None …. nothing …... nada!

She tried a few variations on names, birthdays, anniversaries (no chance!).   She looked in drawers, in notebooks, in his wallet.   He had a list in his wallet, headed Christmas, old and wrinkled, and just about legible.   Sandra – watch (that must have been two years ago!); Amber, new mobile; Sage, deposit for scooter.   Yes, two years, fancy it still being in the wallet.   She read down a bit further and saw Sanbersag – dinner (Rice place)..... She knew that was to remind him to book Ambrosia's – he always called it the Rice place after Ambrosia Rice pudding!   He never had booked it!   They had ended up at the Hawk and Sparrow – nothing wrong with that, but it was certainly not Ambrosina's!   She found that she was crying and put it away and went off to find a tissue and to put on the kettle.   Just silliness.   Solved nothing.

Returning with tea, she went back to trying various combinations for the password, some wacky, some prosaic, some 'Simon likely', some 'Simon unlikely'. You never knew, he might be trying a double bluff! She finally tried 'Sanbersag' and like open sesame the phone sprang into life.   Who would have thought that Simon would have used a combination of their names Sandra, Amber and Sage, as his password.   Not something electronic then.   Just like other people, names of loved ones.   Who said he never remembered anybody's name!

Naturally there was hundreds of emails and texts. She was not sure what to do about them.   Should she just delete all of them.   After all if the phone had been permanently lost, then they would have been obsolete anyway.   With Simon dead, then they were strictly speaking not her business anyway.   Why then had she tried so hard to get into the phone.   What had it all been about?   It seemed so important at the time, but now she had no idea why it even mattered.

She flicked through and as if by some kind of homing device, she saw, not one, but three, separate emails from ..... the National Lottery ..... as she flicked through the hundreds of messages. That was the mystery of the ticket. There was no ticket! Simon had simply used the on-line service. That was why he had just written the numbers down on a scrap of paper! Hardly able to breath, she opened the first one which said those normal words about 'good news' which comes whether you have won £10 or a million pounds, presumably. When she opened the National Lottery on-line, she used the Sanbersag password which miraculously worked again. They had, indeed, won the lottery: £4,000,234.56 to be precise!

She had been almost too afraid to contact them because it was bought on Simon's account and she would be devastated if, as before, the dream was snatched away from her. She need not have worried, and though it was obviously more complicated that it would have been had Simon been staking a claim to the win, and a much longer drawn out process, it was by and large really very straightforward.   It helped that she was able to produce very quickly every possible piece of evidence to prove who she was and why Simon was not claiming the money himself.   She had the Death Certificate, Probate had also now been granted, there was the evidence of a police investigation.   As well as all that, of course, the tragedy of Simon's death had been plastered all over Social Media, in both national and local newspapers, as well as getting mentioned more than once on national and local television news bulletins, so there was no doubt that Simon Jameson was sadly, but decidedly, deceased. They were very sympathetic and mindful of her feelings as a new widow when they asked for proof of death, proof of her identity, etc.   It helped too that the bank account associated with the purchase of the ticket was their joint account, which simplified the process for them greatly.

So, within a few months Sandra had gone from scratching around for enough money to pay the electric bill, to having a new deposit account which had been opened with not only the lottery money, but also an interim payment from the insurers of Kirs Haulage whilst the claim was being fully processed and finalised.

Sandra could relax at last. She felt she had done right by Simon. She had set out to discover what had happened, and she had done so. She was glad, whatever of the sordid goings on around it, that the incident itself was just an accident. It mattered somehow that it was not a deliberate attack, one which Simon would have been aware of and therefore terrified. The suddenness was the only welcome part of the whole horrible thing. The fact that he did not suffer and that he did not have time to know what was happening. Abshir had said it had happened almost instantaneously. They heard the noise, and bang, it was over.

She missed Simon, or more accurately, she missed missing him! She had always been somehow irritated when he was alive by the fact that he was in her house, but never in her life. They had been very different people, but she was sure that they would have grown old together, muddled along like couples do. She would miss that contact, the familiarity, the knowing every frown, every gesture. She only remembered the good times now, and that was the way it should remain.

The lottery win having been reported in particular to show dark clouds do sometimes have silver linings, meant that she suddenly had a call to ask how she was getting along and if she was managing all right from …… Frannie! It's amazing how much more popular she became with her in-laws now that there were several zeros in her bank account! Simon would have been amused – indeed he was probably looking down and chuckling to himself right now.

Epilogue

DI Riley was true to his word and once the whole case had been put together and was ready for trial, he telephoned her to let her know what was happening. He did this not only because he had promised to do so, but also because, assuming the matter went to court, and he was almost sure that the CPS would sanction that, the original story and Simon's death would inevitably get dredged up again, and he wanted her to be warned in advance.

Karl Kirs had been charged with drug smuggling, and amongst those involved in the onward distribution of the drugs was DS Daniels.   It was DS Daniels that Abshir Daud had witnessed arguing with Karl Kirs by the transporter that night, when he met as arranged to pick up a parcel of drugs.   The row had apparently been over the fact that it was the first time that Raymond Daniels had discovered that Kirs was smuggling people as well as drugs. That had been a bit of a 'sideline' organised by Kirs for his own profit and for his eyes only. Abshir was quite right, that particular night Kirs had completely forgotten that he had anybody on board, since it was a last minute arrangement that he agreed to because Abshir offered to pay very handsomely. Kirs normally made sure not to mix the two commodities: if he carried drugs, he did not carry people, and if he carried people, he did not carry drugs. Somehow he felt that this was a safer bet, and the last thing he wanted, or needed, was to get caught with both on board should he get stopped. Apparently Daniels had been livid when Kirs told him, laughingly, as though it was the biggest joke ever, that he had forgotten to let this silly bastard off, and he was giving him grief over it. Said he had no idea what the bloke was talking about because he was did not speak a word of English, but he knew only too well that he was not best pleased. Kirs apparently thought it was very funny and couldn't stop laughing. Daniels did not find it at all amusing!

They had been running the drug importation racket for about 18 months and Kirs used to cross the channel to bring back cars perhaps every ten days or so. He would meet up with Daniels, not every time, but quite frequently, and Daniels knew there were others who were being supplied by Kirs too. Despite the fact that Kirs Senior did not approve of his illegal activities, mostly because it reflected badly on the family and the community, he nonetheless had been harbouring him for the past few months. Local police had kept watch on the place, following a tip off, and they had finally managed to get a photograph of him, through an upstairs window and a warrant enabled them to enter the house and pick him up. He was now in custody on remand. Kirs had wasted no time in naming Daniels as one of his contacts, and two others, one a nightclub bouncer and the other an unemployed former boxer. All three have now been arrested and are in custody awaiting trial.

From what Kirs had said, and the evidence of the police at the scene and the ambulance men, it does seem that Simon's death was a terrible accident.

They would not be able to lay any criminal charges unfortunately. But she should rest assured that they would certainly receive custodial sentences, probably and hopefully substantial custodial sentences for their other crimes.

Sandra, as casually as she could, enquired whether they had caught up with Abshir Daud, but Riley said that they had not, but that his letter to her might be used in evidence to corroborate the story of Raymond Daniels who had decided to give evidence against Karl Kirs in regard to the people trafficking, because he Daniels denies point blank that he knew about, or had anything whatsoever to do with, that part of Kirs' business activities. He seems appalled that anybody should believe him capable of such a thing, though he seems quite resigned to holding his hand up to the distribution and supplying of drugs! I guess even criminals have their standards and some lines that they just will not cross!

Sandra was pleased to have finally got the whole story, and relieved that so far Abshir had not been picked up.

Some months later, she received a letter from Somalia. It was from Abshir to say he was learning English and …...

Dear Madam Jamson,

I write to let you see I learn English and I practice.   I say again thank you for forgiveness that I not return phone so quick.   I hope you now more happy and sorrow time completed for your poor man.   I return home Djibouti safe.   Not caught.   My dear sister now found.   She marry Mr. Price and remain Cardiff.   I now uncle!   I wish you long life and happy days, Madam Jamson.

Yours faithfully, Abshir Daud.

At the end, Abshir had added, like an excited five year

old the following afterthought.

I get gold star for letter. Teacher say it very all right.   I be very able soon.   She say I good quick learner. Goodbye.

THE END

Printed in Great Britain
by Amazon

45130731R00106